"I ought to warn you
my niece is trouble."

Greg's remark was serious but very
quietly spoken.

"It's kind of you to tell me," Renata
said with equal softness.

"But I'm sure you'll cope." He looked
her up and down, a faint smile
touching his lips.

"I'll do my best." She didn't smile. She
kept her eyes steadily on him.
Suddenly tension as sharp and strong
as an electric current filled the space
between them. It wasn't what it
seemed, this conversation. It was a
silent challenge that went from one
to the other. It had nothing to do
with anyone else.

Somehow Renata knew there would
be no letting up. Though she didn't
know why, clearly it was war.

But, she thought, *I'm ready for you,
Greg Masters, whatever you think
about me!*

Other titles by

MARY WIBBERLEY
IN HARLEQUIN PRESENTS

Other titles by

MARY WIBBERLEY
IN HARLEQUIN ROMANCES

Many of these titles, and other titles in the Harlequin
Romance series, are available at your local
bookseller. For a free catalogue listing all available
Harlequin Presents and Harlequin Romances, send
your name and address to:

HARLEQUIN READER SERVICE,
M.P.O. Box 707,
Niagara Falls, N.Y. 14302
Canadian address:
Stratford, Ontario, Canada N5A 6W2

MARY WIBBERLEY

debt of dishonour

Harlequin Books

TORONTO • LONDON • LOS ANGELES • AMSTERDAM
SYDNEY • HAMBURG • PARIS • STOCKHOLM • ATHENS • TOKYO

Harlequin Presents edition published October 1980
ISBN 0-373-10390-5

Original hardcover edition published in 1980
by Mills & Boon Limited

Printed in U.S.A.

CHAPTER ONE

THE bus was slowing. Renata saw the long grey stone wall beginning to her left, so she folded the newspaper and put it in her shoulder bag. They were nearly there. In a minute or two they would be at the main gates, and there she would leave the bus and walk up to Falcon Towers, and begin her new job. And no one would know who she really was, or why she was there, for if they did, they might not have employed her.

'This is it, miss.' The driver looked round as the bus ground to a halt, and the only other occupants, an elderly couple at the front, also looked round and stared at her with the open curiosity of the country dweller.

'Thank you.' She stood up, and as she walked forward the driver left his seat and picked up her suitcase from the cubbyhole behind his compartment, and went down the steps.

'You've a fair walk up there, miss,' he told her sadly. 'It'll be nigh on two mile or more,' and he clicked his teeth and shook his head as if she'd never make it.

Renata smiled. 'I'll manage. Thanks for your help.' She took her case from him and looked towards the huge wrought iron gates with the stone falcons atop each gate-post. The gates stood wide open, as if in welcome. 'It's a nice day for a walk anyway.'

He seemed reluctant to let her go, but she was used to that. 'Aye well, I'd drive t'bus up there myself—but I'd get the sack if I was copped——'

She laughed. 'I wouldn't have *that* on my conscience! It's a nice thought anyway. Thanks again. Goodbye.' She

gave him a last smile and walked to the open gates, aware
that he stood there and watched her. As she went in through
them she turned back and waved, and he waved in return,
more of a salute, and climbed into the bus. Renata stood
and watched it drive away, then it vanished round a bend
in the road, and she was alone for the first time since leaving London seven hours previously.

She took a deep breath. She was here now. It was too late
to turn back even if she wanted to, and she didn't. She began to walk along through the acres of woodland that
stretched either side of the winding drive. Tall trees, and
huge clumps of rhododendrons in full flower, and a kind of
green peace to the air. The sun was bright, but not too hot,
the gravel drive was crunchy underfoot, and there were
arrows on posts at the side, at intervals, pointing the way
to the Towers. She wasn't surprised that they hadn't sent
a car for her. Perhaps they had supposed she would get a
taxi. She gave a wry grin at the thought, and hitched her
shoulder bag higher on her shoulder. She never spent a
penny that wasn't essential, and it was one reason she was
here, and quite ironical, but they'd probably never know
that.

The drive curved to her right, and she wondered if there
were any short cuts for anyone on foot, but there was no
way of knowing that, so she had to follow the road, and the
arrow signs, until she reached her destination. Birds flew
away as she approached, watched her curiously from a distance, then returned to dig undisturbed in the grass. Renata
took a deep breath and began to hum a marching song
under her breath to get into her stride. The slight breeze
made her blue silky cotton dress cling to her, and the full
brightly patterned skirt of it swirled round as she stepped
out, and she was thankful that she had worn her old flat
sandals instead of her one and only pair of high heels for
the long walk.

She might have been in the middle of nowhere. Not a sound, save distant birds chirping in the trees, and not a soul to be seen, and only the arrows to tell her she was going in the right direction. All about her were the trees, and the hilly rise, and the beautiful rhododendrons, and a feeling of calm and peace. She wondered what Falcon Towers would look like, if it would be as huge as she imagined. Of the people living there she thought not at all. There would be time to think about them when she arrived at the front door.

She heard the distant thud of a horse's hooves, but the sound didn't register at first, so engrossed was she in her thoughts, until the noise grew louder, and nearer, and she paused, trying to assess where it was coming from—then saw horse and rider emerge from the trees to her left. She stopped and put down her suitcase—which was growing heavy—and watched the man who approached. He was a big man, on a large chestnut horse, and he was dressed in corduroys and black shirt, and he was dark and tough-looking.

'Hello!' he called, and seemed surprised. He reined in near her on the drive and looked down at her, and she could see, near to, that he was tanned and gipsyish-looking, with shaggy black hair and dark eyes, and she was, for some obscure reason she couldn't explain, frightened of him. Because he seemed like a threat.

She took a deep breath and dismissed the ridiculous fancy. He was an estate worker, obviously, and wondering who she was, to be walking, when quite clearly guests would arrive by car.

'Hello,' she answered.

He dismounted with a grace that spoke of long years' practice, and walked to her. He was one of the tallest men she had ever seen, at least six foot five, and built like an athlete, and his face was hard and as tough-looking as he was—not smiling, not frowning either, but dark and hard, and attractive in a way that she found difficult to look away from. Thick eyebrows met above dark-lashed brown eyes, and his nose was straight and strong, and he had a wide mouth, well shaped, faintly curved as if he had decided to smile and thought better of it, and he needed a shave, which oddly enough did not detract from his tough good looks. But she didn't like him, didn't like the way he stood there as if he owned the place.

'Are you going to the Towers?' he asked.

'Yes, I am.' She didn't like his tone, nor the way he stood there as if assessing her. She was well used to men weighing her up and down, in the street, in shops, just about everywhere she went, but it didn't mean she had to like it. She had developed a cool dismissive gaze. She used it on the man whose dark eyes were scanning her as if searching for hidden weapons. It made her add sharply, sweetly: 'Are you the security guard round here? As you can probably see, I'm not carrying concealed guns.' It was meant to disconcert him, but it didn't. He smiled, but without humour.

'It's unusual to see anyone walking up here. On open days, people come by car. It's not even an open day.' His glance was hard and level, as was his voice.

'The bus dropped me at the gate,' she answered, fighting to control her threatening temper. This man made the hairs prickle at the back of her neck—but she had to be careful. It was essential she stayed here, and she wasn't going to spoil anything by crossing swords with this dark antagonistic man. 'The driver would have brought me to the door, only he had a schedule to keep to.' She smiled pleasantly, coolly at him, and bent to pick up her case. She had no intention of telling *him* who she was, or why she was here.

'Bus? A car was sent to meet you,' he answered, nearly causing her to drop the case.

'A car? What do you mean?' Did he know who she was? Her inner question was answered a moment later.

'You are Miss Page, aren't you?'

She went cold. 'I am. But how did you know?' she said quietly.

'It's logical to assume that as the Towers isn't open to visitors today, and you're carrying a suitcase—which day visitors don't—and are walking up the drive, you've come to stay. And there's only one person expected today, and that's a Miss Renata Page, new employee at Falcon Towers.'

'Quite right,' she answered crisply. 'And now I'll be on my way. I gather I'm on the right route?' She began walking away from him, taking long swinging strides. She had effectively dismissed him. Her first impression, that he had seemed like a threat, was gone. She could cope effectively with any man, and this one would be no exception. She had had to learn how to do so over the past four or five years, when from being a tall skinny teenager she had developed into a woman of almost Junoesque proportions, long-legged, stunning figure, full-breasted, statuesque. That last description had been given to her by a franker, less jealous friend in a rare moment of heart-searching after a party when it had been quite obvious to everybody except Renata that she had caused chaos among the male guests, and dagger-like glances from the females. The party days were over. There was neither time nor money for them, and Renata never regretted the past. She looked only to the future when she would have cleared her late father's debts. Only then would she be satisfied and, perhaps, happy. It was the main reason she was here.

'I'll give you a lift.' The horse had followed her, the man on it, and she looked up at him and smiled. He must think she was a fool. It was a good try. Did he expect her to sit behind him and put her arms round him, or would he seat her in front—and put his arms round *her*?

'No, thanks, I'll walk.'

'Then let me take your case.' He knew, of course he knew. Whatever else he was, he was no fool. But his look gave nothing away. As cool and hard as ever, he surveyed her from the great height of the horse's back, and leaned down.

She handed him her case. 'Thanks.'

'If you'll follow me I'll show you a short cut. It's only half the distance through the trees.'

'No, thanks. I'll stick to the drive.' Where I'm safer, she added, but only to herself. She had had more than one struggle for her honour in dark shady places, and while she was very strong for a woman, she had taken a good look at him, and that was enough for anyone to know that he was possibly twice as strong as the average man. The black shirt he wore was short-sleeved, and his arms were not only long but very muscular, and tanned.

'Suit yourself. Follow the arrows. It's a nice day for a walk.' He gave her a mocking salute, turned the horse's head, and trotted into the trees. There was the crunching of hooves fading, then silence. Renata smiled wryly to herself. She had seen the spark of anger in his eyes, as if he had heard her unspoken words, almost as if she had said them. Then he had gone. She felt shaken, as though she had been through an argument—yet there had been nothing on the surface, only the rippling undercurrents swirling round, and the look on his face and in his eyes, the searching look she was well used to, the assessment—she took a deep breath and started walking the long, long walk to Falcon Towers. She had met one of the staff. She wondered how many more there were, and hoped there were no more like him. She could do without problems like that, she had enough already, and she could hardly ignore the smouldering sexuality he exuded. If he was on the ground staff, it would be fairly easy to keep out of his way, for she would be dividing her days between the elderly Mrs Masters, and her great-granddaughter Christina. She would be earning a lot of money for so doing—and *that* was why she was here.

She hitched her shoulder bag higher on her shoulder. What had he said? That a car had been sent to meet her? She grimaced. The train had got in five minutes early, and the bus had been leaving. She had caught it with moments to spare. She shrugged. No point in worrying about it. She was nearly there now, and the walk was an enjoyable one, even if she had met that man. She strode out, humming under her breath, and tried to put him out of her mind.

At last she saw Falcon Towers as she rounded the final curve in the drive, and she stopped stock still, riveted to the spot, eyes wide with surprise—and something else, more disturbing. The huge sprawling grey stone castle stood some few hundred yards away towering up to the sky, and looking like something out of a fairy tale. Renata had seen a photograph once, but it didn't prepare her for the reality. 'My God!' she whispered, shaken. It was a beautiful building, yet sombre, with the high walls rising to crenellated battlements, behind which were the main buildings. Ivy smothered the tower walls, curving round the long tower windows and creeping up to the very battlements, and high behind them were the towers, the highest of which had a flagpole atop which hung a Union Jack. The drive curved along the side of the building, and to her right was a final, larger post, bearing the words : 'Falcon Towers. Entrance.' She walked slowly nearer, drinking it in, absorbing the frightening beauty of it all. As she neared the outer base walls she could see the small clumps of bright flowers, reds and blues, growing out of cracks in the stonework, softening the strength yet not detracting from it. She took a deep breath. This was larger than she had visualised. There must be literally dozens of rooms in there. There were two doors in the wall, firmly closed.

The man was almost forgotten. Renata walked slowly

along the drive following the side of the building, and saw a copper beech growing almost from under the very walls, curving outwards, the gorgeous red-brown leaves shimmering and rippling in a slight breeze, as if bidding her welcome. She saw a dog running towards her, barking, and stopped.

'Hello, dog,' she said. It was a large black and white rough-haired creature of indeterminate breed, and Renata liked dogs, and liked this one particularly. He rushed, the barks fading as he realised that she was not only not intimidated, but welcoming him, and the long tail began to wag. She bent down to stroke him, and he sat down square in front of her and gave a little appreciative yelp.

'Come on, then. You'd better show me the way in,' she said, and followed him as he trotted back a few feet in front of her in the direction from where he had come. She rounded the curved corner and saw, well ahead, vast gates set in the wall. They were open. The dog ran towards them, barking, tail wagging, and turned to see if she was following.

They opened into a large square cobbled courtyard with stables at the right side, and a trough of water by the far wall. There was a large open door in the left wall into which the dog vanished. Here goes, Renata thought.

Then she saw the man again, and because she had nearly managed to forget him, felt her throat constrict at the memory. He strode across the cobbles from one of the stables towards her. 'You found it all right,' he said.

'I had a nice dog to guide me,' she answered. 'Which way now, please?'

'In there,' he indicated the open door. 'There's another private entrance further along, but you wouldn't know about that. We'll go the long way, and you can see round the ground floor rooms.' He was perfectly civil, but she sensed the undercurrents, the aura of power he exuded, and found it disturbing. 'I took your case in. Mrs Masters is expecting you.'

He led her into a small passage at the end of which was a heavy closed door. The dog sat waiting to be let in, and came back to greet them both. The man patted his head briefly. 'Outside, Toby,' he said. The dog gave Renata a look and then trotted obediently outside. Renata hid a smile. One word from him. . . .

'This way.' He opened the door, and they were in another passage.

'Is this the way guests come in?' she asked, puzzled.

'No.'

'But there's a sign outside——'

'That's for the main doors. They're bolted when it's not an open day. We open on Tuesdays, Thursdays, Saturdays and Sundays. Today is Wednesday, Miss Page.'

'Thank you, I did know that,' she said sweetly, and he laughed. The laugh sent a prickle of resentment right up her spine. She swallowed. He was altogether too sure of himself.

The passage curved round, and ahead were stone steps. 'After you,' he said politely, and it seemed that he could read her thoughts, for his voice had become mock-servile. She climbed the steps. One thing seemed sure about this place: she would never find her way about alone. More corridors, then he opened a large door at the left and they were in the main entrance hall, which was the hugest high-ceilinged room Renata had ever seen, with a desk by a far closed door, and a still, quiet air about it. She looked round, up at the lofty vaulted ceiling with intricate stone carvings looping across. The floor was of stone, and there were crossed swords on the walls, and portraits, and huge settees that looked as if they hadn't been moved for centuries, covered in dark red material, heavily and intricately patterned. There was a recessed fireplace nearly as big as a normal room, and inside, baskets of logs in the hearth. She shivered slightly, for it was cool here in contrast to the warm sun outside, and wondered how they had ever managed to heat it in the old days.

'Needless to say, these rooms aren't used nowadays,' he said, and she wondered if he could read her mind, or had seen her shiver.

'This one is rather large,' she admitted.

'There are more. Come.' She followed him along into a banqueting hall, with a polished slate floor, and a long table stretching from one end to the other. The sunlight filtered through in many-coloured facets via high stained glass windows depicting knights and their ladies. Renata felt the sense of history, and absorbed the beauty as she slowly gazed round her, awed into silence. And the man watched her, but she was scarcely aware of him, only of the feeling of timelessness here, of an age long gone.

'Ready?' The mocking, careless voice broke the spell. She turned.

'Yes.' She would see it another time, without him. This would mean nothing to him. Why should it if he was used to seeing it nearly every day? He might be employed as a guide as well as whatever else he did.

'Do you want to see more, or shall I take you to see Mrs Masters?'

'Take me to Mrs Masters, please. It's bad manners to arrive late—I didn't know about the car, of course.' She turned to him. 'I'll look round some other time, I think.' Without you, she thought.

He nodded. 'This way, then.' He led her back to the corridor, through a door marked Private and up more curving stone stairs. Then they were in a different world altogether. It was like stepping out of history into a modern age, taking a step from past to present.

The man took her down a wide carpeted passage with

doors opening off at either side, and a long skylight letting in golden sunlight. He tapped, then opened a heavy door on their left and ushered her in. She was in a large comfortably furnished living room, with long settee and chairs covered in flowered chintz, antique furniture that shone with the loving care it received, and large french windows opening out on to a small flagged terrace.

An elderly woman sat in a chair by the window, a tapestry frame on her knee. She was slim, white-haired, with a beautiful serene fine-boned face, and she wore a plain black dress upon which was pinned a diamond star-shaped brooch. She smiled at Renata and extended a long thin hand.

'Welcome, my dear. I'm Florence Masters. Forgive me not getting up, but——' she gestured towards two walking sticks at the side of her chair as Renata crossed the carpet towards her and took the proffered hand.

'Mrs Masters, I'm sorry I'm late. The train was a few minutes early and I caught a bus.' She looked round at the doorway, where the man stood.

'I know. Greg told me.' Greg—so that was his name. But still Renata didn't realise. 'You must have a drink straight away. What a long walk! And how I envy you being able to do it.' And she smiled. The smile transformed her face, and Renata saw that she had once been a very beautiful woman, and still was. Her bone structure was perfect.

'Do sit down. Tea or coffee?'

'Coffee, please.' Renata sat in a tapestried chair a few feet from her employer.

'Greg, ask Peggy to come in, will you, dear? Are you stopping?'

'No, thanks, I've got some jobs to do. Your suitcase is in your room, Miss Page. *Au revoir.*' He went out and closed the door, and Renata looked at her employer, trying to hide herconfusion. The casual manner in which both had spoken to each other was not what she had imagined it would be between employer and staff.

Florence Masters leaned back and surveyed Renata. 'Well now,' she said, 'here you are. How fortunate you met Greg! Having to carry a case two miles up that drive must be no joke. Although I'm annoyed about the car. I assumed you'd know we'd send someone to meet you.'

Renata smiled apologetically. 'I'm sorry,' she answered.

'Don't apologise! Heavens, we should have made it clear in the letter. But I'm delighted to see the agency picked someone so obviously right for the job. Your work won't be arduous—but it could be a strain for you in some ways. My great-granddaughter Christina is at a difficult age, I'm afraid—fourteen—' she sighed. 'She needs firm discipline, which I, because of my handicap, am unable always to supply. She has a tutor every morning, but in the afternoons I would like you to assume full responsibility for her, accompany her to York and various places, take her horse riding, swimming, playing tennis. She's been a problem since her parents were killed, and more so recently now she's growing into womanhood. She needs companionship and guidance, and the agency assured me you were ideal for the job.'

'I was a nanny to a diplomat's family in Paris for two years, until they returned to America,' Renata said. 'There were three boys, and they'd been allowed to get away with murder.' She smiled.

'And?' Mrs Masters eyes widened, as if fascinated.

A grin broke out on Renata's face. 'They were well behaved when I left. Mrs Damero, the diplomat's wife, asked me to go back to the States with them, but I had to refuse, unfortunately.' Because Mr Damero had been paying too much unwelcome attention, and was proving even more difficult than his sons had been at first, she thought wryly.

'How did you do it?' The older woman's face reflected Renata's grin. 'How on *earth* did you manage?'

Renata shrugged. 'There was no set pattern really. I suppose I went by instinct. It seemed to work.' She gave her employer a lovely warm smile. 'I understand children—I sometimes feel like a child myself, perhaps that's why. And I can remember my own childhood problems. Just give me a little time, that's all I ask, and I'll do my best.'

The older woman looked shrewdly at her. 'You also got this job because of your qualifications in sports,' she said. 'I was most impressed.' Renata smiled modestly. There seemed nothing to say. 'Did you really play tennis for your county?'

'When I was fifteen, yes. And I swam for England when I was sixteen.'

'Good heavens! They didn't tell me that. I'm even more impressed.'

'Please don't be. I was just lucky. With two older brothers I'd always been a tomboy, simply to be allowed to play with them! It's very good training, I assure you.'

Mrs Masters laughed. 'Oh, I think we're going to get along very well. You have a refreshing honesty about you that I like. Good——' the door opened and a girl popped her head in. 'Oh, Peggy, two coffee, please.'

'Yes'm.' The door closed again. Mrs Masters smiled at Renata. 'Then I'll take you to your room, and after dinner you'll meet Christina. She's sulking in her room at the moment, because one thing she *doesn't* want is another bossy woman making her work—her words, not mine.'

'Oh, I see.' There would be problems there. But Renata knew she would cope, because she always did. She had coped ever since her father died, a bankrupt, leaving many debts that she had dedicated herself to paying off. She had worked hard, scrimped and saved every penny for the last six years, and was well on her way to her goal. And the main creditor had been the Masters family, for whom she was now going to work. Only they didn't know that, and it seemed a poetic kind of justice that they shouldn't. She looked up as the older woman spoke. 'Greg's away so often, you see. She adores him, of course—but then, apart from me, he's her only relative.'

CHAPTER TWO

THE words seemed to echo and re-echo round the room. Renata sat very still, trying to hide the shock that filled her. Greg—the man who had met her in the drive. The man whom she had thought an estate worker—Greg—the rough, tough-looking horseman who made her hackles rise simply by the way he spoke and looked at her, was a member of the family who had helped to bankrupt her father!

'My dear, what is it? You've gone white!'

She looked up. 'I'm sorry. Nothing. I—you must think I'm very foolish. I thought he—Greg—worked here. Your words took me by surprise, that's all.' The bad moment had passed. All was well again. Renata had had too many surprises in her young life not to have learned to hide them. She remembered only too well the prickle, the sensation of fear she had experienced at their first meeting. It had not been a false one. If he found out who she was—if he guessed—she shivered, then pulled herself together and smiled at the older woman. She had no quarrel with her. It was her son, Nicholas Masters, who had run the company, that had caused all the trouble. And now there was something she had to know.

'Is he—Mr Masters—your son?'

'Heavens! Greg, you mean? No. My grandson. He's Christina's uncle.'

'I see.' So Greg was the son of Nicholas Masters. He might even be in the same business. Mrs Masters had said something—just before the shock—about him being away so often. On business? Better not to ask. Not yet. She had to tread carefully. The man she had met so briefly, first in the drive and then in the courtyard, was very shrewd as well as being tough.

Something had changed in the atmosphere. Renata could see that the older woman was slightly puzzled, but there was nothing she could do about it. She was still absorbing the shocks, wondering if there would be more. Her brain was busily working. It was a relief when the girl returned with a tray with coffee and scones on it, and left it there, and the next few moments were occupied with pouring out the coffee. Renata took advantage of it to change the subject.

'And in the morning I'll be helping you,' she said.

'That's right. I do so love to get out in the gardens, and while Greg will always help me—when he's here—and one of the staff when he's not, it's always so much nicer to have someone with you to chat to, isn't it?'

'Of course. I'll enjoy that.' She had been prepared not to like her new employer, been prepared for a rich spoilt old woman, but the money was too good to allow any consideration like that to mar it. And meeting Florence Masters had been a genuinely pleasant surprise. There must be a catch in it somewhere. It must be Christina. She was probably utterly revolting. Renata thought quietly: but I'll deal with her. I won't allow her to ruin my chance of earning the best money I've ever been offered. Two years, saving everything, and the amount in the bank, gathering interest, would be sufficient for her to go to the Bankruptcy Court and apply to have her father's memory cleared. It was a burning ambition that had consumed her ever since he died, and Renata, once determined on a course of action, followed it through. Which was why she wouldn't allow either the girl or her uncle to stop her fulfilling her plans. She drank her coffee and hid the growing sense of conviction of the rightness of what she was doing. She would earn her money, and would make sure she earned it.

She had had her doubts on the journey, doubts about the necessary deception involved. She had even taken her mother's maiden surname to avoid any recognition of her own name before she was ready to reveal it. Her brother Jerry, working in America, didn't even know of her plan. Her other brother, Neil, thought she was mad, and had frequently told her so, but he was reckless, like her father had been, and a gambler, and she had sworn him to secrecy over this job. And James Harlow—he too thought her mad, but knew better than to argue with her once her mind was made up. Renata was uncomfortably aware that he was too obsessed with her to do more than make a token protest at her decision. He had sworn he would phone her every day, come up and see her once a month, and write in between times, and she was well aware that he would. He had not liked her changing her surname. With his precise lawyer's mind, he knew that while not strictly illegal, it smacked of deceit. He loved her, and was possessive—but Renata didn't love him, and knew she never would. She liked him, she was even very fond of him, in a sisterly way, but how could she fall for a man who took life so seriously? James, alas, was one of those unfortunate people who possess no sense of humour. He laughed politely at jokes, when in company, but never really understood them. His saving grace, in Renata's eyes, was that he was a good friend to Neil; in fact Neil had introduced them. And she supposed, now, as she allowed the events to pass through her mind, that she had in a sense used James. She had encouraged him—not that he had needed any encouragement, simply so that he would stay friendly with Neil and—she swallowed at the thought, but she was being very honest with herself—keep him out of trouble. She sighed, and then, suddenly embarrassed, was aware that Mrs Masters was watching her intently, half smiling.

'Oh, do forgive me!' she gasped.

The older woman laughed. 'My dear, you were miles away, completely lost in thought.'

'I'm so sorry. We were talking about going in the grounds each morning—provided it's fine, of course. But I do know there's a covered swimming pool here. Mrs Masters, have you ever had water therapy suggested to you?' She was making up for her lapse in manners, but she had had an idea as well, and if it would help, she would make time to do it.

'Since my fall, you mean?' The agency had told Renata that Mrs Masters had been badly injured in a fall from a horse seven years previously.

'Yes.'

'Well, they took me in the pool when I was in hospital having therapy, but it was special spa water. What exactly do you mean?'

'I've got a friend who teaches at a school for handicapped children and adults. She takes some very bad cases in the water for remedial exercises—and of course, as we're all comparatively weightless in water it's so much easier for them to do. It can be of tremendous help.'

'But I'm seventy-three, my dear!'

'Can you swim? Or rather, could you?'

'Well, of course, but——'

Renata smiled. 'Please. May I telephone my friend?'

'Well, of course you may. But you intrigue me strangely. Wait—watch me walk.' The old lady fumbled for her sticks and Renata leapt forward, but Mrs Masters stopped her.

'No, let me get up myself. I'm not being awkward, I prefer it. Then, if you still think you can help, telephone your friend.'

Renata subsided into the chair and watched, biting her lip, as Mrs Masters struggled to get up, and succeeded after a few moments of what seemed to be great pain. Then she walked slowly, and with obvious difficulty, towards the door. Renata observed her closely, seeing the tautness of her grip on the walking sticks, the way her right leg dragged, the awkward line of her hip. She felt sympathy and a sense of sadness. She cared deeply about people, and suffering, no matter whom, and she cared about this woman, whose courage was undoubted.

Mrs Masters manoeuvred herself round and walked slowly back. Then she sat down. After she had got her breath she said: 'Well?'

'I'm sure my friend can help.' Renata's eyes shone. 'She can tell me what she advises, then you can ask your doctor, of course, then I can take you in the pool every day—or whenever you wish. Is the water heated?'

'Yes.' Suddenly Mrs Masters laughed. 'You're a very determined young woman, you know that? You're sweeping me along in a kind of wave——'

'Oh, I'm sorry——'

'Sorry!' She banged her stick on the carpet. 'Sorry? I'm not sorry, so don't dare apologise again! I think it's marvellous!' Her eyes twinkled. 'Phone your friend, my dear—may I call you Renata?'

'Of course, please do.'

'It's a lovely name. The telephone is in the corner. I shall wait.' She held out her hand as Renata stood up. 'Wait, let me tell you something before you do. Whatever your friend says—whether it's practical or no—thank you for the thought. Now, off you go.'

It was nearly five; Diana would be at home. Renata picked up the receiver and dialled, well aware that she would have been able to speak more freely with no one in the room, but she had no choice. As she dialled, Greg Masters entered the room. She had her back to him, but she knew who it was. It was almost as if a tingle leapt up her spine and she knew without turning round that he was looking at her. His grandmother's words confirmed it.

'Renata's only phoning a friend of hers, Greg. I'll wait until she comes off and then tell you what it's all about.'

His voice was low, but Renata, listening to the ringing tones as the telephone shrilled in Diana's flat, heard him clearly. 'You seem very lively, Grandmother. What are you cooking up?' His voice faintly amused, humouring her.

'You'll see——' She stopped as Renata answered her friend's hello.

The conversation was brief—but during the course of it, when Renata realised what was going to happen, she went cold. As soon as she could, she thanked Diana, said she'd be in touch, said goodbye, and hung up. She *had* to telephone her again, as soon as possible—and privately. For Diana, full of helpful suggestions, and clearly delighted at being asked, had said immediately that she would post off a book that might help to Renata that evening. But Diana didn't know of Renata's change of surname, and would send the package to Miss Renata Strachan. And there was no way she could tell her during that conversation—especially not with him there.

'Look, may I go and make a call—a private phone call, please? I'll pay, of course——'

'Of course you may. Greg, take Renata along to her room. You have a telephone there, my dear. Make as many calls as you like.'

'It won't take a minute, then I'll be back and tell you what my friend said, only this is rather important——' She found, to her horror, that she was babbling. Worse, Greg Masters was watching her with an amused, almost knowing expression on his face—although he couldn't know——

'Off you go, then.'

Greg held the door to the passage open. 'This way, Miss Page,' he said.

'Renata,' his grandmother's voice followed him, and he smiled.

'Of course—Renata.' But he was smiling at his grandmother, not at her. The passage widened into a square hallway with a wide stone staircase leading down, and portraits lining the walls. There were several doors, and another passage leading off.

'The stairs lead down to the public part,' he said, as he led her into the second passage. 'They're roped off at the bottom on open days, so no one comes up. Your bedroom is the fourth room along here. The first is my grandmother's, the second my niece Christina's, and the third one mine.' He smiled slightly at her, but all the time he was watching her. All the time, until she felt like screaming, telling him to stop—for this was subtly different from the usual male scrutiny. It was deeper, searching, and she felt as though he was able to probe into the innermost, secret recesses of her mind and know what was there.

He opened the door. There was a long interval between doors in that passageway, and she knew why when she saw the bedroom. It was not only large, but there was another door leading off into what was obviously a bathroom. Modern and light, the floor was carpeted by a very expensive-looking Chinese carpet, delicately patterned in fawns, pinks and greens, and there was a large modern fourposter bed with fluffy pink candlewick bedspread. A telephone stood on the bedside table, and to this he pointed.

'Your phone.'

'Thank you. It's a lovely room.'

'Yes, we like to look after our guests. I hope you know what you're doing,' he added, without a change of tone, which made his remark more devastating. Renata stared at him, heart thumping, eyes wide.

'What?' The word came out rather faintly.

'With my grandmother. I couldn't help hearing your conversation.'

'Oh!' Relief flooded through her. For a moment....

'I hardly think you can do anything the doctors haven't thought of.'

She had regained her briefly shaken composure. 'I wouldn't dream of going against experts. I just think it's possible to help.' She regarded him coolly, watching him as he put her case by a small table near the window. It wasn't her imagination—but he wasn't looking at her, assessing her, in the normal male way she had grown accustomed to. He made her feel uneasy in a far different way, which she didn't fully understand. He was a strange man, an unusual man, not in the conventional mould at all. Until she got the measure of him she must play it very cool. Renata smiled to herself as he opened the windows at the top. And what better time to begin than now?

'Thank you so much,' she said. 'Sometimes windows are difficult to open,' she gave a feminine, helpless shrug. 'Going back to what you said, Mr Masters, I shall not of course dream about trying anything without consulting you and Mrs Masters—only I once helped the friend I telephoned, when she took some children away for a few days. I enjoy swimming, and went along more as an extra "hand" than anything, but I was surprised at how mobile people can be in water—as long as they're well supported.' She went over to the chair at the other side of her bedside table and eased off her sandals, while looking at him with an 'aren't I a helpless little thing?' look in her beautiful blue eyes. 'Do forgive me taking off my sandals. I enjoyed the walk—but you were so right, it was a long way!' And she smiled, and rubbed her ankle, and managed to give the impression of soft feminine helplessness.

'Make yourself at home,' he said dryly, face straight. His

expression gave nothing away. 'I'll be with my grandmother in the lounge when you're ready.'

'Thank you, Mr Masters. I'll only be a few minutes.'

He went over to the door. 'I suggest you call me Greg,' he remarked. Renata blushed prettily, a trick that had served her well in the past, and looked slightly confused.

'Th-that's very kind of you——'

'I'm sure Grandmother would expect it,' he cut in smoothly. 'You seem to have made a very good impression on her. I'll see you in a few minutes—Renata.' And out he went, closing the door.

Renata sat back in her chair and let out her breath in a long, silent, 'phew!' She gazed up at the ceiling, seeing his mocking face, hearing the words again. Was it her over-active imagination, or was everything he said double-edged? And if so, why?

She picked up the telephone and began to dial. First things first. She would puzzle about Greg Masters later. She explained to Diana the necessity of addressing the letter to her in her new surname, and Diana, who was one of those rare friends who accepted everything with equanimity, agreed. Renata had only just been in time. Diana was going out soon after, and was already preparing the brief letter to accompany the book. Renata thanked her again and hung up, then made a quick call to Neil to let him know she had arrived safely, and gave him the number.

Then she went into the bathroom, compact, pink-tiled from floor to ceiling, with two fluffy pink bath towels on a heated rail, and washed her face and hands. She was ready. She slipped on her sandals, grinning at the words she had said. She could have walked ten more miles without tiring. She wished, briefly and only fleetingly, that she possessed more glamorous clothes. It was not a thing that had ever bothered her before. She had grown so used to scrimping and saving, and making her own dresses from market stall bargain remnants, that the thought was almost alien—but she felt instinctively that she needed a few weapons in her armoury. She shrugged, and promptly forgot about it as she left the bedroom.

She smoothed her glorious tumble of dark brown hair just before she knocked on the lounge door. Not much she could do to keep it in order. She had very thick hair, naturally curly, and five minutes after even a vigorous brushing, it was as unruly as ever. Men seemed to love it. . . .

'Please come in. You don't have to knock, my dear.' Greg had opened the door, and his grandmother's voice chided her gently as she entered the room. 'Did you make your call all right?'

'Yes, thanks. I wanted to let my brother know I'd arrived safely.' And that was no lie. Renata was basically truthful, and was glad she had telephoned him, even if only as an afterthought.

'Now then, come and sit down and tell me what your friend had to say.'

'Excuse me, won't you?' Greg stood by the door out, and his grandmother waved an impatient hand.

'Off you go, dear. I do hope you'll change before dinner?'

He looked down at his casual attire and grinned. 'Would I let you down, Grandmama?'

She snorted. 'You'd probably forget all about it—I know you!'

'Then I'd better escape now before you fill me with shame.' He blew a kiss at the older woman and went out, laughing.

Renata sat quite still. He was a very attractive man. The thought had just struck her, belatedly, and with the force of a blow. The toughness only accentuated the virile aura that surrounded him. She felt an inner tremor. He looked very strong——

'Ah, men!' Florence Masters sighed, but with a smile. 'They're like little boys, aren't they?'

Tact was called for. Renata laughed. 'I have a friend, a very staid and respectable lawyer, who still has his train set from boyhood. I know what you mean. Sometimes I suspect he'd like to set it out and play with it—but he denies it, of course.'

'Your boy-friend?' Florence Masters put her hand to her mouth. 'Oh! How nosey of me!'

'It's all right,' Renata smiled. 'He is, in a way——' She paused.

'Tut! It's none of my business! Only—may I say it—you're a very striking-looking young woman, my dear. And so tall—oh, there I go again! I was very tall when I was younger and I was always very self-conscious about it those days, but now—well, it's lovely to see all these tall young women about.' She looked at Renata with a little smile.

'I was always the tallest in my class,' Renata agreed. 'And very skinny. Now I enjoy being tall, I must admit.'

'Hmm. D'you know, I've got a collection of old evening dresses from the twenties. A beautiful collection, including some of those fabulous Fortuni dresses—I dare say you've heard of them——'

'Heard of them? They're *super*. And they're fetching huge amounts these days. They're the ones you screw up to put away, aren't they? I always thought it was like sacrilege until I saw photos of some in a Sunday paper supplement.'

Florence Masters laughed. 'There you are—I thought you'd know. We really must have a look through everything one day when you have time. I'm sure some of my dresses will fit you perfectly—I'd love you to try them on.'

'I'd love to try them on as well.' Renata gave a slight smile at the thought, which recalled her own as she had left her bathroom. 'I make all my own clothes, and that's a bit predictable——'

'Good heavens! Did you make that one?'

'Yes.' Renata looked down at it, and smoothed the cotton skirt thoughtfully. 'It only took me a few hours, just a simple pattern——'

'But how clever! I was thinking how expensive it looked.'

Renata laughed. 'Under a fiver!' She was beginning to like Florence Masters more with each passing minute. She was probably only being tactful and polite—but she did it with a genuine air of pleasure, and there was not the slightest trace of snobbery about her. And it was at that very moment that Renata had the first very faint stirrings of conscience about the deception she had embarked on. For there was no other way to describe it. She had sought, and got, the job of companion to this elderly woman, and as semi-teacher to her great-granddaughter, in the sure knowledge that they wouldn't have dreamt of employing her had they known who she really was. Which was why she had used her mother's surname. The money was excellent, on a level with the high salary she had enjoyed in Paris. And in a way she was only taking it so that she could pay it back....

It didn't alter the fact. She looked at the older woman, and for a moment the impulse to tell the absolute truth, and face the consequences, was so strong that she opened her mouth to speak, to tell her——

The door crashed open and a bundle of energy erupted into the room. Renata looked round, startled—and saw it change into a very tall, skinny girl wearing tattered jeans and dirty faded blue tee-shirt. 'Granny!' the girl said accusingly, then stopped, and glared at Renata. 'Oh!' She subsided into a sullen, smouldering silence.

'Renata dear, this is Christina,' said Florence Masters calmly, just as though the girl had walked in quietly.

'Hello, Christina,' she said.

It was an effort, you could see, but the girl managed it. 'Hello,' she muttered. Her expression was anything but welcoming, and on a par with her appearance, which only just escaped being scruffy. Her black hair was long and slightly greasy, she was barefoot, and the jeans might have been jumble sale rejects. Her arms were long and thin, as were her legs and body, and Renata remembered, with a pang, how she herself had been built at that age. Her pale freckled face barely escaped a scowl. Her one saving grace was brown, thickly lashed eyes—like her uncle's.

Renata caught Florence Masters' eye, and the look she gave said it all. 'There, I told you didn't I?' that look said, almost as if she had spoken. But when she spoke, her actual words were very different. 'What is it, Christina?'

'Oh, nothing. I'll see you later.' She shuffled uncomfortably and Renata stood up.

'I really ought to go and unpack,' she said with a smile. 'If you'll excuse me?' A glance of understanding was exchanged with the older woman, who nodded.

'Of course.' Renata went quietly out. She had to pass Christina, who seemed to shrink away and freeze as she did so. She closed the door, and heard, faintly:

'Really, darling, do you have to rush in like that?' and the even fainter reply as she moved towards the bedrooms:

'You know I don't want *her*—I don't want anyone——' Anything more was lost. Renata was out of earshot—perhaps, she thought wryly, just as well. Miss Christina Masters was going to be a handful, to put it mildly, if expression was anything to go by. There had been defiance in every inch of her face.

Renata unpacked her meagre collection of clothes into wardrobe and drawers and sat down on the bed. What now? It was no use rushing back too soon if Mrs Masters and Christina were still talking. She went over to the window and looked out at the spectacular view of rolling acres of trees merging in the distance with the hills. It was a beautiful day, and the lush greens blended and merged into one glorious blur of colours, from somewhere a long way in the distance a tractor engine droned, the faintest scent of cut grass came in through the open window, and Renata closed her eyes, remembering. . . .

It had been like this once, with them, once long ago, living in a large house—nowhere near the size of this, of course—with large rolling lawns and trees. Those days had long gone. Renata shared an apartment on the outskirts of London with two other girls, and had worked very hard for the past year as secretary during the day, and helping out with a friend's catering business during the evenings. The friend, Pam, ran a rather superior 'meals on wheels' service for dinner parties to the wealthy. It was on one of these jobs that Renata had overheard a conversation that had led her to Falcon Towers.

Pam was sorry to see her go. Renata serving a meal was a sure guarantee of success to any dinner party, especially an all-male affair where the men wouldn't be concentrating on the food so much as gazing at the server of it. Her boss at the secretarial agency, Jack Hedges, had been equally regretful, had assured her that she was to let him know the moment she decided the country life was not for her, and watched her go, sighing deeply.

Renata, remembering this, smiled slightly to herself. Jack Hedges, a divorced man in his middle forties, had always been asking her out—and once or twice, on a rare free evening, she had gone. She knew with an inner certainty that she could have, with only minimal encouragement on her part, made him propose to her—but she had no intention of getting married. Not now, not ever. She had seen too many unhappy marriages to want to join the ranks of bitter women and hard-faced men.

She possessed tremendous energy, and when the debts

of honour were finally paid she intended to work her way round the world while she was young enough to enjoy the challenge. She drew herself up to her full height and looked calmly out of the window. She would do it, she knew she would. She also possessed, as well as abundant energy, a quiet confidence in her own ability to do anything she wanted.

It was time to go back. They had had sufficient time to talk, and Renata wanted to make a clear plan of her daily tasks as soon as possible. She was on a month's trial. That had been implicit in the interview at the agency that Mrs Masters had employed to find the right woman for the job. She had a month to make herself indispensable—and for that month, she knew she would be wise to avoid Greg Masters as much as possible. Renata had never met a man like him. Normally of an even temperament, she had discovered, to her dismay, that he had an odd effect on her. He made her hackles rise simply by his presence, let alone his soft barbed words. She had never met a man she wanted to hit before. . . .

She chuckled at the thought, took a deep breath, and went out into the corridor to walk back to the lounge, and to Mrs Masters. And the first person she saw was Greg, emerging from his room. He had changed, and shaved. She didn't know how he had done it in the time, but he had. He wore a casual white rollnecked sweater in a thin silky material that clung to him, emphasising his muscular build; and slim-fitting black corduroy jeans. Oh, *machismo!* she thought. The arrogant male showing off his muscles to impress the little woman. Well, I'm not impressed. She looked calmly at him and smiled. She would smile, come what may, for the next month. . . .

'I've just been to unpack,' she said. 'Ought I to change now?'

'I don't think it's necessary,' he said smoothly, and fell into step beside her. 'That dress is quite suitable for dinner. My attire wasn't. And in any case I'm going out immediately afterwards.'

Whoopee, she thought. Bully for you. Am I supposed to be impressed by that as well? 'Oh, I see.' She wondered if he expected her to ask where he was going, in which case he would be disappointed. She had no intention of doing so.

'Do you ever go out in the evenings, Renata?' he asked.

She looked at him. 'Not a lot,' she answered. 'And I'm here to work, of course.' The words were softened with her special gentle smile.

'Not in the evenings, you're not,' he said, and, no mistaking it, there was that mocking edge to his voice, the one that had the effect on her. They were in the wide hallway now, with the stairway leading down, and she turned to him and laughed.

'I suppose not. I hadn't thought about it.'

'Then you must. My grandmother will certainly expect you to have time off in the evenings—and at weekends, of course.'

'Of course. That's something we'll discuss. I've only been here an hour or so, Mr Masters——'

'Greg.'

'Oh, I'm sorry, I forgot,' she apologised gracefully. She hadn't forgotten at all, she had done it deliberately. 'Greg. It would seem rather—presumptuous of me to begin asking about my time off when I've not even started work, wouldn't it?'

'No.' He looked coolly at her, and stopped. They were only yards away from the lounge now. Renata stopped as well. 'You seem to me to be the sort of young woman who is prepared to state exactly what she wants.'

'Do I?' She gazed at him with an insolent air. 'Good gracious!'

The corner of his mouth quirked. 'Yes,' he said, and began to walk on again. Oh God, don't let me hit him, she prayed silently. She was disturbed by her own strong reaction to him. She wanted to reach out, to swing him round —she caught her breath, and walked, as calmly as she could, after him; her hands were shaking, and she was afraid, because how could she be calm and cool ond indispensable when he was around?

He paused before opening the door. Faint voices could be heard from within, and he turned to Renata. 'I think I hear my niece,' he remarked, quite as if they had just been having a pleasant chat—which, on the surface, was all it had been.

'Yes. We met before I went to unpack,' she managed to answer.

'Ah.' He raised one eyebrow. The 'ah' and the lifted eyebrow both carried a deeper meaning, and Renata thought she knew what it was, a thought confirmed by his next remark, very quietly spoken as if to avoid any possibility of being overheard. 'Perhaps I ought to warn you that Christina can be—er—difficult.'

'It's kind of you to tell me,' she said, equally softly.

'But I'm sure you'll cope.' He looked her steadily up and down, and a faint half smile touched his mouth.

'I'll do my best.' She didn't smile. She kept her eyes as steadily on him. Suddenly tension, as sharp and strong as an electric current, filled the space between them, and she caught her breath in her throat. It wasn't on the surface at all, this conversation. It went far beyond the conventional words they spoke. It was a silent challenge that went between them, and had nothing to do with anyone else at all. Greg Masters turned away to open the door, and it all seemed to be happening in slow motion, she knew with a deep inner certainty that there would be no letting up on his part. She didn't know why, or how it had happened, but it was war. But I'm ready for you, she thought.

CHAPTER THREE

GREG indicated that she was to go in first. He held open the door and Renata walked past, thanking him with a smile. Christina stood by the window looking out, her back defiant, and Florence Masters gave Renata a sharp look, then shook her head slightly.

'I'm going out after dinner, Grandmother,' said Greg, as if unaware of anything amiss in the atmosphere.

'That's nice, dear. Anywhere special?'

'Virginia's got some friends she wants us to go to.'

'Oh! Try not to wake me up when you come in——'

'As if I would!' He grinned amiably and crossed over to his niece at the window, and tweaked her hair. 'Why don't you show Miss Page the swimming pool, Chris?'

'I've got some homework to do,' was the muttered, barely audible answer.

'Have you now? Miss Taylor decided to make you work a bit harder, has she? That won't do you any harm. But it won't take ten minutes—so off you go. I want to talk to your grandmother.'

For a moment Renata, standing just inside the doorway, thought the girl was going to refuse, and she wondered what would happen if she did. Surely a man like Greg Masters wouldn't bow to a child's tantrums? Then she heard the added word from Greg: 'Now.' It was very quiet, but it brooked no refusal.

It was sufficient. Christina turned and stared at Renata. 'I'll show you the swimming pool,' she said in a flat little voice.

'Thank you, I'd like that.' Renata opened the door again

36

and went out, and waited. Christina came out.

'This way,' she said, and led her towards the large landing, and down the stairs. Renata followed, perfectly content not to speak—yet. She would wait her time.

It wasn't long coming. As they went across a small hallway with stone walls, and towards a narrow passage to an outer door, Christina turned. 'I may as well tell you now,' she said. 'I don't need *anyone* to teach me soppy things like tennis and swimming—and *you'll* be wasting your time staying.'

They were near the outer door now. Renata nodded, but said nothing, and Christina, after a moment in which it was clear that she didn't know if Renata had heard, opened it, and they went out into a grassy square, walled on two sides by the building, and at the third and fourth by a low stone wall in which was a small gate. They reached it and went through, and ahead of them was what looked like a domed conservatory, the glass faintly steamed up. Renata was busily wondering how Mrs Masters could be taken down there without too much difficulty, and came back to the present with a start as Christina added: 'Didn't you hear what I said?'

'Yes, I heard.' Renata smiled at her, a friendly disarming smile. 'Ah, is this the only door?'

Christina opened it. 'There's another one on the far side,' she glowered. There was a full sized swimming pool, surrounded by green tiles, the water shimmering and dancing in the sunlight striking in through the glass. The air was very warm and humid. At the far end were several changing cubicles and a foot bath. Renata looked round, pleased with the pool, and then at Christina.

'Now, what were you saying?' she asked. 'Something about not wanting me here?' She inclined her head pleasantly, waiting for the answer. It had the disconcerting effect she had intended. Christina was now going to have to repeat her words—with the knowledge that *they* hadn't had the effect *she* had intended.

She saw the girl swallow, and felt quite sorry for her. There was also something else she intended to find out, something she felt sure she hadn't been told. 'I don't want —I mean, I don't *need* anyone here in the afternoons— I'm quite happy on my own——'

'You don't look it,' said Renata very softly, and she smiled gently.

'You've no right——' the girl burst out, her eyes blazing with temper.

'Listen, Christina, we're alone now. You're obviously going to say what you like—and so will I. When your uncle suggested you show me the pool I was pleased, because after talking to your grandmother I decided I could help her—in the pool—by letting her do exercises. Now, I'm not only here to teach you things you couldn't care less about— I'm here to be a kind of companion to your grandmother, and that I intend to do to the best of my ability. Whether you like me or not is entirely up to you—you'd already decided you wouldn't before I came, which is slightly unfair —but that's not important to me. I'm quite sure you've already made snap judgements before—how many others have been employed here, doing what I'm doing?'

Christina, stunned, looked at her. 'There was Miss Rivers last year——' she muttered at last, reluctantly.

'And what happened to her?' Renata said crisply. Her guess had been right. 'Did you manage to scare her off?'

A spark of sheer devilment lit the girl's eyes, and seeing it, Renata went on before she could speak: 'I can see you did. What a clever girl that makes you, doesn't it? I won't ask if there were any more. I don't really want to know, because I don't give a damn. I'll just tell you this, now, while we're alone. I don't scare easily. I don't know what methods you used with her, or them—whether it was just overwhelming rudeness, the kind you're displaying now, or whether it was little tricks—oh yes, I've been fourteen once, you know, and I also looked after three boys who'd knock you into a cocked hat for bad behaviour—and I'm not afraid of spiders or mice or frogs or things that go bump in the night, and they tried them all, believe me.' She paused, to let what she was saying sink in, before she delivered the *coup de grâce*. 'And if you want to go round looking like an Oxfam reject, that's okay by me. Do you look like this all the time, or did you put that lot on for my benefit?'

'Oh. *Oh*!' Christina stamped her foot, burst into tears, and rushed out. The door swung to behind her, and Renata gave a deep sigh and sank down on to a bench at the side of the pool. She imagined no one had ever spoken to the girl like that before. She had taken a gamble, and all she could do now was wait and see what happened. But it was a calculated risk, based on the despair she had seen on Florence Masters' face, and the quiet tone of Greg when he had insisted he be obeyed. She had had to do what she had, establish herself right at the beginning, or life would have become impossible. She crossed her fingers, then got up and went out into the sunshine. There was a bench near the gate in the outer wall. She sat down, opened her bag, and began to write in her diary.

She hadn't long to wait. She heard a door opening, then footsteps on the grass, and looked up to see the gate opening. It was, of course, Greg. He looked across at her, and it was hard to tell if he was angry or amused.

'Congratulations,' he said dryly. 'You've reduced Christina to tears, and after giving us a garbled horror story she rushed off to her room.' He sat down beside her. 'Would you care to tell me your version?'

'Certainly,' she looked at him calmly. 'But before I do, would you mind telling me how many others there have been—*before* Miss Rivers, I mean?'

'*Touché.*' He nodded as if in acknowledgment. 'There

were two, as a matter of fact. She told you, did she?'

'No, I guessed. Now, my version. Do you really want to hear it? I mean, she is your niece, and I'm a stranger. I'm sure I know where your loyalties lie.'

'Chris can be—and frequently is—a pain in the neck. Much as I love her, I'd be the first to admit that. So yes, I do want to hear what you said to her.'

'Then I'll tell you.' And she did, practically word for word. He listened intently, not once interrupting, and there was for the moment nothing of the arrogance and mockery she had so quickly become aware of. It was as if a truce—for the time being anyway—existed.

When she had finished he nodded, as if surprised. 'I see.'

'And am I fired?' Renata asked flippantly. But she knew, she knew already—her gamble had paid off. She could see it by what was in his face.

'You've done the right thing,' he said. 'You socked it to her all right. Are you like this with everybody you meet?' And as he said it, it was there again. The tension was there, imperceptibly building up.

'Only if they ask for it,' she retorted smoothly. 'And if it's necessary. Instinct told me to get my piece in first, so I did.' She glanced sideways at him, calm and composed because in spite of the fact that he had a primitive spine-tingling effect on her, and she could feel the tension subtly shimmering beneath the surface, she had won an important first round. 'Is that what you were waiting for—is that why you asked Christina to take me to the pool?'

'I don't understand your question.' But he did. He knew all right.

'I think you knew she'd be rude. Did you hope to see me come back a quivering wreck?'

He laughed. 'What a fascinating picture you conjure up!'

'You haven't answered the question.'

'I thought you might as well know what you're up against——'

'Because she takes after you?' she said lightly.

His eyes went cold and hard. 'What *do* you mean?' he asked softly.

She smiled. 'I think you already know, Mr Masters—oh, I'm sorry, Greg.' She inclined her head.

'Perhaps I ought to remind you that you are a member of the staff,' he said.

'I shan't forget it, don't worry.' She stood up and smoothed down her skirt. 'May I go back now?'

He stood up as well. They were facing each other, and he really was overpoweringly tall, close too. And very intimidating. 'Be careful, little Miss—Page.' He seemed to hesitate over her surname, but it could have been her imagination.

'Thank you,' she bobbed a mock curtsey. 'It's not often I'm called "little".' She looked up very slowly, from his waist upwards, as if it took her a great deal of time. 'Nobody could call you that, could they?'

'Miss Page? Hardly,' he answered dryly.

'I meant—little.' She didn't know why she was behaving so recklessly, so out of character. She was going against everything she had promised herself, yet it was as if she couldn't help herself. Nobody had ever had this effect on her before, and it *was* frightening, and she would have to think about it later, but she was being carried along by the power of the moment, a force beyond her own understanding. It was because he was like he was, and a silent challenge had been issued, and accepted, and there was nothing she could do about it for the moment. She tried to escape, to break the spell by moving away, but he caught her arm.

'Don't run,' he said. 'Dear me, don't run away now.'

'I'm not running away!' she snapped. She could feel the strength of the fingers gripping her arm and she wanted to rip his hand away—to strike out—she caught her breath. Stop it, she thought. *Stop* it—her breathing was rapid. She felt breathless.

'It seemed like it. Do I scare you?' The subtle mockery was back.

'No one scares me,' she whispered. 'Not even you.'

'No?' He laughed. 'That's good, You've had enough—shocks—for one day.'

'Please take your hand off my arm,' she said quietly.

He did so, lingeringly, his fingers sliding away very slowly. 'Mmm——' he smiled his crooked smile, 'I should think you're very strong—for a woman.' Their eyes met and clashed, and neither looked away. The vibrations made the rest of the world seem very still, almost meaningless, almost—non-existent. Only two pairs of eyes, one blue, one brown, that met and locked in the continuation of the unspoken challenge that didn't need to be spoken. It was there—strongly.

'Strong enough,' Renata murmured, 'to look after myself.'

'Yes, I can see that.' The words seemed meaningless, almost. They were mouthings to conceal what was really going on. Renata felt almost dizzy, and knew with sure feminine instinct that Greg was also affected. How, she didn't know, but he was.

'And have you always been so—positive?' he drawled.

'Is that the word you use? Is that how you see me? Because I don't allow a teenager to lay the law down—or you to assault me?'

'Assault?' He lingered over the word. 'Touching your arm?'

'Yes. In a way.' Her face felt cold. It seemed as if it were a mask she wore to hide her true feelings, of her reaction to him. 'How would you feel if I took your arm like that—prevented you from moving? You wouldn't like it.'

He narrowed his eyes. She saw a muscle move in his jaw, saw him breathing as though he had been running—or was angry. 'Do you always have an answer?'

'Not always.' She lifted her chin slightly. 'Won't Mrs Masters be wondering where we are?'

'Probably.' He half turned, and as he did so, looked back, and down at her; it was like an electric shock coursing through her. 'Yes, we had better go, before we say something we might—regret.'

She was free to move, released by his moving. Her limbs felt heavy, as if she had just emerged from deep water. She walked towards the gate, and he pushed it open, and she said, 'Thank you,' as she walked through it. Greg followed, and closed it; it was all like a dream, slightly off balance, not quite right, yet in no way she could put her finger on. They walked across the grassy square, and everything seemed bright and sharp and clear, and she looked round her in surprise at the very clarity of everything. Suddenly Greg Masters said:

'Why have you come here?'

She paused. They were nearly there, nearly at the door. 'Why?' she repeated. 'I needed a job, that was it. Why else?' She looked at him.

'How did you hear of it?' he said.

It was time to be cautious, not to give too much away. Not to admit she had heard the name Masters and taken it from there, shamelessly eavesdropping to find the name of the agency that were interviewing prospective employees. 'I used to help a friend who ran an outside catering service for dinner parties. Someone at one of the dinners told me Mrs Masters needed a companion for herself and for her great-granddaughter. I went to the agency and got the job. That's all.'

'Did you know we'd had thirty applicants before you?'

'No, they didn't tell me that.' She gave an inward smile. Over thirty!

'And you got it.'

'Someone had to,' she pointed out, quite reasonably she thought.

'True. Did you know anyone at the agency?'

'No,' She turned round slowly. 'What are you trying to say? That I got it by pulling strings or something? I promise you I didn't.' She stared at him and he nodded as if in acknowledgement.

'I'm sure—when they interviewed you—they realised.'

'Realised what? They put me through it, I can tell you that. You'd have thought I was after a job guarding the Crown Jewels!'

'Realised that you'd do.'

'And is that what you think?' She tilted her head. 'Or do you have doubts?'

'You've dealt effectively with a mixed-up teenager. Let's see how you go on.'

'I'm on a month's trial. At the end of four weeks, if I'm not satisfactory, I'll have to go. They made that quite clear.' She opened her eyes wide.

'But you'll have to stay,' he said softly. 'Won't you?'

'I think I will.' Had it gone cold, or was it her imagination? She felt a shiver run through her and goose pimples on her arms.

'Cold?' he asked.

'It is getting cooler.'

'Then we'll go in.' He pushed open the door. For a few yards they were in the darkness before the hallway, and it was instantly colder. Renata felt his presence beside her, a potent force, reaching out to touch her almost like a physical touch, and she moved quickly to escape, because she was no longer sure of anything, so confused did he make her, but he mustn't know that. He caught her arm again, only this time it was gentle 'Careful—mind the bench,' he said, and when she nearly fell over the concealed seat there he pulled her away from it, towards him. For a moment, just an infinitesimal second of time, she allowed it to happen, her senses dulled with the contrast of shadow after light, and it seemed to happen in slow motion, as though that second lasted for ever. . . .

Her body touched his, and it was fire and life and heartbeats mingling, then it was over. Renata found her balance and Greg held her a moment longer and said: 'I didn't want you to fall—not in your first hours here.' The words seemed to come from far away, far away——

'Yes,' she said, breathless. 'Thank you.'

It was over. It had been nothing. A man who knew a dark place, stopping someone from stumbling. No more.

Then they were in the stone hallway, and the stairs were there, and everything was quite normal. Renata smoothed an errant curl from her forehead. 'What time is dinner?' she asked.

'In about——' he studied his watch, 'half an hour. Hungry?'

'Fairly.' She was able to speak normally now. They were nearly back in the world of sanity, of a sweet gentle old lady and an awkward girl who both needed help. And nothing had happened. Nothing had *happened*. Except words, and looks, and a smouldering meaningless conversation she could scarcely remember, only the hidden words that could never be said, and eyes that couldn't look away, and a man who was disturbing and frightening and powerful all at once. And she had never known anything like this before.

'We have a very good cook,' he told her. 'Her husband's the chauffeur.'

'The one who went to the station?'

'The very same.'

'Oh dear, I'm sorry about that.'

'Not your fault.' They walked side by side up the stairs. 'These things happen.'

'Yes.' She wanted them to be not alone. She wanted to be in the room with Mrs Masters, and safe.

And, moments later, they were. Of Christina there was no sign, but Florence Masters stood by the window, leaning on her sticks, looking out over the estate. She turned slowly when Renata went in, followed by Greg, and Renata went over straight away to her.

Greg spoke before either woman could. 'It's all right, Grandmother,' he said, and his voice was soothing, very reassuring. 'Renata merely told Chris a few little home truths that should have been said long ago. You're not to worry, do you hear me?'

Florence Masters gave a wry smile. 'That's easy for you to say, my dear,' she said.

'And true. Wait, I'm going to have a few words——'

'No!' She moved painfully forward.

'Yes—now. I'll be back, don't worry. Just remember—I love her as much as you do.' He had gone, even as he said the words.

Renata helped the old lady to her chair. 'I'm sorry,' she said. 'I had to say what I did, or it would have been no use me staying.'

'I know, I know, my dear. She was upset when she returned, but I knew—I sensed—she'd had a shock. Oh, Renata!' she sighed. 'She's such a problem. I thought, when I saw you, that you'd be ideal, but when she rushed in, I was so upset——'

'I'm sorry.' Renata held the other woman's hand. 'Please believe me—I know what I'm doing.'

'Do you? Do you really?' The old woman's eyes were bright and anxious.

'Yes. There were others, weren't there? No one had told me.'

'Yes.' Florence Masters seemed to slump. 'What—did you say?'

Renata told her, gently and carefully, and Florence Masters listened as Greg had, intently, silent.

'Ah! No wonder—thank you for telling me.' She managed a smile. 'You did right.' She squeezed Renata's hand. 'Let's hope it works.'

Amen to that, thought Renata. And now, so confused was she, she doubted. Which only made what happened afterwards so much more of a surprise.

The dining room was behind one of the doors leading off from the wide landing. Renata and Mrs Masters made their way there. Of Greg and his niece, there was no sign. They went in, to where a long table had been set for four, and Renata helped Mrs Masters to sit. It was seven o'clock. What now? she thought. Do we wait? She looked anxiously at the older woman sitting regally at one end of the table. The maid popped her head in. 'Shall we serve dinner, 'm?' she asked.

'Please, Peggy.' Mrs Masters inclined her head, and the girl vanished. And then came the miracle. A few moments later the door opened again and in walked Christina, followed by Greg. It was a new Christina. Gone were the old jeans and scruffy tee-shirt, in their place a simple blue dress, and her hair was tied back with a ribbon. She looked as though she had had a good wash as well. She went straight over to her great-grandmother and kissed her on the cheek. Renata sat holding her breath. She couldn't have moved or spoken if she had wanted to.

Florence Masters smiled very gently. 'Just in time, you two,' she said. 'I'm glad you've put that dress on, Christina, it's one I particularly like.' She turned to Renata as the other two sat down. 'Tell me, Renata, this friend of yours, Diana I think you said, has she been teaching for long?'

It was a gentle conversational gambit, and it was done with a purpose. Renata took her cue promptly. 'For about five years. She's a little older than me—I admire her tremendously for her dedication.'

'I'm sure. Does she work in London?'

The conversation was established. The incident at the swimming pool might never have happened, nor afterwards. Greg joined in, then Christina, with a tentative question regarding the kind of teaching Diana did, and during this the maid entered with soup, and Renata answered, smiling at Christina, telling her of an amusing incident involving Diana and the time she had gone with a party of children to visit a stately home, and one had got lost—and the dinner passed in a pleasant atmosphere.

Then it was over. They made their way back to the lounge, Greg helping his grandmother, Renata and Christina following, side by side, not speaking, but the hostile atmosphere wasn't there anymore. When Mrs Masters was seated comfortably in an easy chair near the television, Greg bent to kiss her. 'I'm going out now,' he said. 'Don't wait up—I'm a big boy.'

She tapped his hand. 'Give my regards to Virginia. Have a nice time.'

'I will.' He straightened, and looked at Renata who waited to be told to sit down. Christina had curled up on a cushion on the carpet, watching him. 'Don't stay up too late. And be good.' He gave a wave that might have been meant for Renata, but was possibly for his niece, and went out.

'Do sit down, make yourself comfortable. We're going to watch that serial on BBC1—I hope you'll like it.'

'Oh, the one about parapsychologists? Yes, I've been watching it,' said Renata, seating herself comfortably. She had seen part of one episode at least, and it had looked good. She was quite happy to go along with whatever the older woman decided. It was time to relax, and unwind, and let everything happen naturally. She sat back as the screen flickered into life and the title music began. She wondered what Greg had said to Christina. She would never know, but it was interesting to speculate. Whatever it was, it had worked. The girl was silent, but not sullen. She watched the screen intently, engrossed in the serial unfolding before them. Where had he gone? To visit friends with someone called Virginia, he had said. His girl-friend—fiancée—mistress? Renata thought about it. She wondered what Virginia looked like. Not that she cared, of course, or was even remotely interested—but she thought about what kind of woman would attract a man like Greg Masters. Petite—tall? Certainly slim and elegant. Blonde, brunette, redhead? She touched her own hair, scarcely aware of what she was doing. She could almost picture her. Hard, brittle, smooth-faced, well made up but cleverly, subtly—witty? Perhaps. She wondered what kind of place they were going to. Greg was dressed very casually. They would be at someone's house, and it would be crowded, and he would have a drink in his hand, and tell Virginia about the new woman who'd arrived—she could almost hear his words, the amusement in his voice.

She found she was clenching her hands tightly, and relaxed consciously as the serial unfolded. What did it matter? Greg and his affairs had nothing to do with her, nothing at all. She didn't like him, and he didn't like her, it was clear on both sides, but he wasn't important in her scheme of things. The two important people were here, now, sitting watching a television screen, engrossed.

The serial over, the music began for the news, and Florence Masters looked round at Renata. 'Well now,' she said. 'That was certainly good, wasn't it?'

'It was.' But she couldn't have said what had happened, if asked. She had been unaware of what had unfolded, engrossed in her own thoughts. Christina rose, picking up her cushion. She looked briefly at Renata.

'Scrabble, Granny?'

Oh, not tonight, dear, I'm very tired. Renata, can you play Scrabble?'

Renata looked at Christina, judging the child's reaction. She seemed to be waiting tensely for her reply. 'I've not played for ages, to be honest.' She looked at the girl and smiled. 'I'm sure you'll beat me.'

The girl's eyes pleaded for something, Renata knew not what, but her heart ached in sympathy. She had left it to Christina. Either way....

'I'm not very good either.' Christina smiled, actually smiled in return. It was a mere twitching of the lips, very unsure—but it tried.

'Then we'll be well matched,' Renata grinned. 'Let's see, shall we?'

Without a word the girl went out, and the older woman looked at Renata. 'Oh, my dear, you're doing very well,' she said softly.

Renata raised her right hand, fingers crossed. 'Just wish me luck,' she answered equally quietly.

'I will.'

Christina returned with the box, space was cleared on the table by the window, and while Florence Masters watched the news intently—or at least appeared to be doing so—Renata helped the girl set out the board and letter racks, and shake the letters in the canvas bag. Renata intended losing—but not by a wide margin, which meant a subtle cleverness was called for. It would be a good way of assessing Christina's general intelligence as well.

She realised after only minutes that she was going to have her work cut out if she wasn't going to lose ingloriously. Christina not only knew obscure words, she had the knack of getting the top value letters. Right, thought Renata, and put all her concentration to this new challenge. The girl played to win—and so did Renata. Anything else would be an insult to the girl's intelligence, which was very high.

When it was over, the scores totted up, and Christina had won by a respectable margin, Renata looked at her accusingly. 'I thought you said you weren't very good? Hah! I've never even *heard* of quiddany—and I thought my vocabulary was good.'

'It's a sort of quince jam,' said Christina. If she was feeling pleased, she managed to hide it. There's still a long way to go, thought Renata, but the ice is getting a little thinner. She grinned at the girl.

'Okay, let's have another one, shall we? This time, I warn you, it's war!'

Florence Masters looked round. 'Need a referee?' She was smiling.

'No, thanks. What I need is a dictionary!'

They began to play again, and this time Renata was in top gear. Any less than her best effort would be an insult to Christina, who, whatever her faults, was a shrewd player. This time Renata scraped a win by five points, then sighed.

'Phew! That was close, but I enjoyed it. Do you play chess, Christina?'

'Yes. Do you?'

'I do—but I'll warn you now, I'm quite good.' She was putting it modestly. She was very good.

'So'm I.'

'Want a game?' Renata asked casually.

'Can I, Gran?'

'Just one—as long as it doesn't take too long.'

Christina rushed out, and Renata said quietly: 'I think we're both learning.'

'Bless you! She's a very bright child, Renata. Play your best, she enjoys a challenge.'

'If she plays chess as well as she plays Scrabble, I'll need to. She's very intelligent.'

Christina returned, the board was set out, and play began. The maid came in with hot drinks and biscuits, but they were scarcely aware of it. The concentration needed excluded everything else. Time passed, Mrs Masters switched off the television and came over to tell them she was going to bed, and both girls looked up blankly, and seeing this, the older woman smiled, and shook her head. 'Not too late, mind,' she said.

'No, Gran.' The girl looked back at the board, and Renata smiled. She might not be winning at chess, but she was winning another battle.

CHAPTER FOUR

By the time the game was finished over an hour later, and both sat back exhausted, Renata thought she knew so much more about Christina that would explain the girl's bad behaviour and resentment. The game of Scrabble had started a train of thought that the chess had confirmed. Christina was of an exceptionally high intelligence, far greater than her years.

'You outmanoeuvred me all the way,' Renata admitted. 'Christina, have you ever done any I.Q. tests?'

'No.' The girl looked at her suspiciously. 'Why?'

'I'll tell you in a moment. Can I ask you something personal?'

The girl shrugged. 'What?' warily.

'What kind of marks do you get in your schoolwork?'

She flushed. 'Average,' she muttered. 'Why?'

' 'Cos I'll tell you something——' Renata had to choose her words carefully. Any hint at patronage or flattery would send the girl back in her shell quicker than insults. She took a deep breath. 'I've realised something while we've been playing. You've got a brilliant brain—and I'll bet any money you're not using it.' Christina sat very still, not saying a word. Here goes, thought Renata. Take the plunge. 'Does your tutor tell you you're lazy?'

'Yes.' It was a mutter.

'And careless?'

Christina looked up, eyes bright. 'So what?' Defiance in every inch of her.

Renata nodded calmly. 'I knew it.'

'Huh, you're so *clever*, aren't you?'

'Yes, I am—and so are you. Only you hide it. Why?'

'What does it matter? Nothing matters.'

Renata banged the table, making Christina start. 'Damn it, yes *it does*! Intelligence like yours is a gift a lot of people would give their right arms to have—and you're wasting yours. Wasting it, do you hear?'

She indicated the board and the Scrabble box. 'These games don't even try you to the full. You skated through. I had to really concentrate to win that second game of Scrabble—and I'm older than you, and I know a lot of words—but I only won because I was lucky. Now I know you don't like me, or want me here, and quite frankly, I don't blame you—because if you can play tennis and swim as well as you can play these you don't need anybody to teach you anything—*you* could teach others—but please don't ever say it doesn't matter.'

Renata's eyes sparkled; not with anger, but with the desire to communicate some of her own enthusiasm for living to the young, unhappy girl who sat shocked and silent opposite her at the table. It was another gamble, another challenge, and Renata, as was her way, met it head on. 'Because it does matter—not the winning so much, but the way you go about it. I'll tell you something I've never told anyone before. When I was fourteen I went through a stage of not caring. I was lazy, rude, insolent—and it showed in my work. There was a very good teacher at my school, a kindly woman—as I'd always thought, quite easy-going. I thought I could get away with it, because, like you, I couldn't care less. And one day—I'll never forget this— she took me to one side, in a quiet room, and she told me.' Renata sat back and lifted her eyes ceilingwards. 'Boy, did she tell me! She tongue-lashed me—she wiped the *floor* with me. And when she'd finished I could have crawled out from that room under the door with room to spare. But it worked. I never again tried anything on anybody.'

She paused, and smiled gently. 'You see, Christina, she told me what I'm trying to tell you. She told me that I had a good natural intelligence, a God-given gift, and I was throwing it away with my defiance and rudeness. I never forgot her words, and just a few years ago I wrote to thank her for what she'd done—only the letter was returned by her sister. My teacher had died only months before, after a long illness. So she never knew how much I appreciated her telling off—and I regret that very much.'

Christina picked away at a loose thread in the cloth that covered the table. Her head was down. She would not meet Renata's eyes. Renata watched her, saw the tremor in the too thin body, knew that for the moment, the girl literally couldn't speak or look, and was quietly satisfied. She had nearly finished. Very gently she said: 'I'm on a month's trial here, as I'm sure everyone else has been. Shall we decide, now, that it's going to be a fair trial on both sides?'

There was a long silence, but she knew better than to break it. Then, slowly, Christina raised her head. Her eyes glittered with tears. 'A month?' she said.

'Yes. Just four weeks in which I'll do my best. Will you do yours?'

The girl nodded, and Renata held out her hand. 'Shall we shake hands on that?'

Almost shyly, Christina held her hand out and they shook solemnly. Renata took a deep breath. 'I think we ought to celebrate,' she said, grinning at the girl. 'But I forgot to bring any champagne with me—even if I'd been able to afford a bottle!'

Christina looked round. 'There's some sherry in the cupboard.'

'Sherry? How lovely!' Renata hated the stuff.

'Gran lets me have some sometimes.'

'Then let's have a drop, shall we?'

Christina went and opened a sideboard and came back

with two glasses and a decanter. As she put them down, she said: 'What did you mean about I.Q. tests?'

'Oh, those!' Renata had forgotten her question about them. 'You know, the usual thing. The average I.Q. is 100. A university student would have one of—say—130—and then, for exceptionally clever people, there's a society called Mensa——'

'Are you in it?'

'Thanks for the compliment, but no! I'm not even sure how clever you have to be. Something astronomical, I'd imagine. I bet you'd waltz in.'

Christina looked shocked again, and Renata said: 'I'm not joking. Do you think I am? I never joke about serious things. You have a gifted brain. I think, while we're sipping the sherry, we might just have a little talk about you, and what you really like doing.' She raised the glass. 'Cheers, Christina.'

'Cheers.' The word didn't come easily, but she was making an effort.

The sherry was very dry and light, and a pleasant surprise to the palate. 'Now, please tell me—if you want to, that is, if there's anything you'd like to do as well as—or instead of—tennis and swimming, etcetera.' Renata made her tone deliberately brisk and businesslike, then picked up the leaflet with the rules of the Scrabble game on casually and studied it as though she'd never read it before.

Christina took a deep breath. Renata didn't look up. 'Do you speak French, Renata?'

She looked up then, smiling. 'I worked in Paris for two years, with those boys—didn't I tell you that? Yes, I do. Why?'

'Can I tell you in a minute?'

'Sure.' She waited, casual, glancing at the leaflet. There was all the time in the world. . . .

'And can you ride a bike?'

Renata tried to hide her surprise. 'Yes.' What on earth next?

'And can you speak Dutch and German?'

'Ah. Dutch, no, alas—but German, a smattering, yes. Enough to get by anyway. Christina, you've got me delightfully confused. Are you going to tell me why you want to know before I burst with curiosity?'

The girl grinned, actually *grinned*. 'All right, I will. First, French—I learn that from Miss Thing, but she's a bit—well, old, and—well, what I mean is, can we talk in French sometimes? I mean, have proper French conversations?'

'It's as good as done. You want to start *now*?'

'No.' Christina shook her head. 'Perhaps tomorrow, if you don't mind.'

'Right. And the bike?'

'Can you teach me to ride one?'

'I'll do my best. Why not? Have you got one?'

'No.'

'Hmm. Slight problem. Still, I'll talk to your grandmother. Next—Dutch and German.'

'Well, I want to—well, I'd like to be an air hostess when I'm older, and you need languages, you see, and I thought——' she stopped, as if suddenly realising she was pouring her heart out to a stranger she didn't want or intend to like.

Unhurriedly, Renata said: 'I've always wanted to learn Dutch, funnily enough, but I've never had time. You know, we could send for one of those Linguaphone courses. It could be fun if we both learn together—that would really put us on our mettle, wouldn't it?' She laughed. 'As for German, a few books should refresh my memory. Any good bookshops near here?'

'York.'

'Right. Say, why don't we go there tomorrow? Would

your grandmother let us—in the afternoon, I mean? I've not been there for years. I seem to remember there are a lot of good bookshops in the old Shambles too.'

Christina's eyes lit up. 'Do you *like* bookshops?'

'*Like* them?' Renata laughed. 'Try and keep me away!' She sobered. 'Do *you*?'

Christina nodded. 'Oh *yes*!'

'Really, truly?'

'Yes.'

'Have you got many books, Christina?'

'Mmm. In my room. I've got bookshelves lining one wall.'

'Good grief! Can I see some time?'

'Yes.'

'And whom do you read, mainly?'

The girl rattled off a list of authors—mainly adult— that astounded Renata by the range and scope of subjects covered. There were many of her favourites too, Daphne du Maurier, Monica Dickens, Dorothy L. Sayers, Ray Bradbury, O. Henry, Charlotte Brontë—Renata was silenced.

She put her hand to her forehead when Christina had finished. 'I don't believe it,' she said faintly. 'All my favourites, and more besides. You must *eat* books! I thought I was a reader, but you've beaten me hollow.' She shook her head. 'That's amazing, really. I'll bet you started reading when you were about four, didn't you?'

'Mmm.' The girl nodded, eyes alive for the first time.

'Snap! So did I. Joined the local library at five—if you could write your name on the form, you could join. So I practised for *days* to get it right.' Christina laughed. 'And then I toddled in—with my mother, of course—and got out my first two books. Andrew Lang's *Lilac Fairy Book*, and an Enid Blyton. I was so *proud*—of course, I could hardly read a word of them—I should have been getting Dr Seuss or something similar, but oh no, I knew I wanted *proper* books, none of your kid's stuff. My elder brother ended up reading most of the stories to me—not very graciously, I might add—but I didn't care. I was a reader.'

She shook with silent laughter at the memory, and Christina joined in—as Greg walked through the door.

To say he looked astonished would have been an understatement of magnificent proportions. He looked *stunned*. But only for a moment. In fact Renata was the only one who saw that brief flash of stupefaction before it was replaced by amusement. 'Is this a private joke or can anyone join in?' he asked.

Christina looked at him. 'It's nothing really. We were talking about books.'

'Books. Ah, I see. Yes, a great cause for merriment, I always say, books.' He looked at the sherry decanter. 'Hmm, I *see*,' he added.

'No, you don't.' Christina jumped up and hugged him, and breathed on him. 'See? I've only had a drop.'

He lifted her from the floor as though she were light as a feather, and swung her round. 'Don't give me that, little minx. You and Renata have been getting quietly sloshed while I've been out.'

Renata watched. It was obvious that the girl and her uncle had a good easy relationship. It was also time for her to withdraw tactfully. She was still the stranger. Christina might close up, feel that she had lost face if it seemed that Renata was getting on too well after the girl's resistance.

She stood up. 'I really think I'd better go to bed,' she said. 'Please excuse me, I'm rather tired after the journey. Thank you for the drink, Christina. Goodnight.'

She smiled at them both and went out, hearing their goodnights following. Why was Greg in? He had set out for the evening. She smiled a little smile to herself. Perhaps the lovely Virginia had found another boy-friend. Not that

I care, she thought. Not that I care at all. But she was curious.

She wondered, as she prepared for bed, what the other bedrooms were like, and if there were more guest bedrooms in that part of the house. It was still unfamiliar territory to her, but there would be time to explore, plenty of time later. She heard no sounds of Christina coming to bed, but the walls were so thick that the rooms were virtually soundproof.

Renata put on her nightdress, a simple yellow cotton one she had made herself in an evening, opened the bed, and climbed in. She made a little murmur of appreciation. This was how a bed should be! Firm mattress, two huge soft pillows, and sheets of smooth blue cotton that smelt faintly of lavender. She sat back and pulled up the duvet, then picked up the magazines someone had left for her on the bedside table. Three glossy monthlies, very heavy, very expensive, of the kind she never bought, but read in the dentist's waiting room at her twice-yearly check. She settled comfortably to read the first *Harpers and Queen*. The window was open, and a slight cooling breeze rippled the curtains, and she was snug and warm, and the print blurred and danced. She closed her eyes, just for a minute to see how comfortable the bed really was. . . .

When she woke up it was morning. She hadn't remembered putting the light off, that was the strange thing, but it was off. And she hadn't remembered replacing the heavy magazines on the bedside table, but they were there. She hadn't remembered anything after closing her eyes, only for a moment. She must have fallen asleep. It was nearly seven o'clock. Renata always woke at that time, regardless of how late she had gone to bed the previous night. Time to explore, alone before breakfast, if she could find her way down. Mrs Masters had told her she was free to wander anywhere she liked, and Renata intended to do just that, before the hordes of visitors descended.

Within fifteen minutes she was showered, dressed and ready to go. She never had any problems with make-up, because she never wore any. She gave her hair a vigorous brushing, took a brief glance at herself in the mirror, smoothed down the tight jeans—very tight jeans—she wore, wondered if James would approve of the equally snug-fitting blue sleeveless sun top—he wouldn't—and grinned at her reflection. James wasn't here. And if Mrs Masters didn't approve, she would change it. It promised to be a scorching day, and Renata hoped that Mrs Masters would want to go out in the gardens, for she loved the sun.

She was ready. She crept out, down the corridor, down the stairs, and out through the tiny dark passage—careful to avoid the bench—and into the grassy enclosure. Now where? At the gate she stopped and looked around her. Not a soul in sight, not a sound to be heard except the birdsong from the trees. She stretched her arms out. Oh, it was good to be alive! Then she set off towards the trees. She loved walking in woodland as well, and these trees were tall and thick and very old, and the ground underfoot was crunchy with long dead leaves and twigs. A hedgehog scurried away, and a quick flash of movement, a darting shape flee-ing up a tree, was a squirrel. Renata nearly laughed out loud because she was alone, and happy, and she hadn't stopped to think why, it was simply because.

The ground sloped gently down, the trees thicker than ever, and it was like being in a jungle. Not a steamy jungle, but a cool, civilised English one, with the sun completely cut off, only the dark greens and browns blending in a glori-ous shadowy moving kaleidoscope. She reached the edge of the trees, and what lay ahead was so unexpected, so sudden, that she stopped to get a proper look, to take it all in. Be-low her, sloping gently away, was a hidden valley, with a river running through it, and the sunlight slanting in, still low, at an angle; small trees and shrubs dotted the slope, and it was achingly beautiful and simple, and it seemed as if no one else had ever been here, so quiet and secret was it. Renata looked back towards the trees from which she had emerged. They effectively hid everything. She could have been miles away from anywhere—perhaps she was. It was easy for imagination to run riot. At the far side of the river the ground sloped upwards again, and there was more woodland.

Renata decided to follow the river for a while and scrambled down towards it, dislodging small stones which clattered down towards the bank. She wore her flat sandals, which made walking easier, reached the grassy bank and bent to run her fingers in the water. It was icy cold. And it was at that moment she sensed she was being watched. It was no more than an awareness, a vague tingle at the back of her neck. She stood up and looked around. Nothing moved, only the leaves on the trees stirred in the faintest of breezes. She was alone, of course she was. Who else would be mad enough to get up at seven and go exploring? She didn't feel nervous anyway, only mildly curious. She set off walking along the twisting side of the river; could see well ahead of her now, and the river curved away into the distance, towards more trees, so that it appeared as if it was in the wood itself. She hadn't the faintest idea where it originated, but as long as it didn't take too much time, she intended to find out. It grew cooler as she neared the trees, and a bird skimmed along the water, soared upwards and vanished.

The river emerged from the woodland, and there were rhododendrons, and azalea bushes lining its banks and the ground sloped upwards again so that she was climbing away from it, leaving her beautiful little river behind. It would be difficult to stay by its banks, for there were large rocks, which would mean climbing and scrambling over them. Perhaps she would come with Christina some time and do it then. She stood and watched it from her slope, then sat down, plucked a long blade of grass, and began to chew it. The sensation returned, of being watched. Renata glanced round casually.

It was eerie. She wasn't nervous, but she felt the faintest prickle of unease, the merest frisson, and that simply because it was annoying not to be *sure*. She looked at her watch. Nearly eight. It would be sensible to go back now anyway. She had been out for half an hour, so it would take her that long to reach the Towers, breakfast was at nine, and she was *starving*.

She took a last lingering look at the cool rippling water, turned round and began to strike upwards towards the trees. Someone called her name, and she didn't need three guesses to know who it was. She shaded her eyes and looked round the vast expanse of greens and shadows. Sound was deceptive here. The trees could muffle the sound or distort the origin. She saw nothing. If he was playing a trick, it was a stupid one, she thought, and began walking again.

There was the clatter of hooves, and Greg emerged from the trees she had left behind and he and the large horse made their way towards her. The horse picked his way delicately across the sloping pebble-strewn hillside. Greg rode it bareback.

He reined in and dismounted. 'Out early, aren't you?'

'Yes. And you.' She smiled. She had decided already how she was going to behave towards him, and she intended to stick to it. The trouble was he was very disconcerting, close to. He wore jeans as slim-fitting as hers. They were old and faded, unlike hers, and if she had had any doubt about his muscular legs before, she didn't have now. He wore a red checked shirt, and a leather belt at his waist; his hair was still wet, as though he had just washed it, and his face was hard and cool, and giving nothing away.

'Exploring the estates?'

'Yes. I like walking when no one's about. I thought some-one was watching me about a quarter of an hour ago.'

'Is that why you decided to turn back?'

'No.' She laughed. 'Why should I?'

'Why indeed?' he murmured. 'You're going in the wrong direction.'

'No, I'm——' she stopped, looked around, frowned. 'Am I?'

'Yes. Keep on walking that way and you'll land up by the main gates,'

'Well, fancy that!' She bent to ease a tiny pebble from her sandal. 'It's a good job I saw you, then. Thanks for tell-ing me. If you point me in the right direction I'll be on my way——'

'No need. Hop up behind me, we'll ride back together.'

Now it was absurd, because Renata didn't like him, but she felt the strangest tingling sensation when he said that. Almost like the feeling she'd had when she thought some-one was watching, but that had been down her spine. This was all over, and for a moment it was almost like being lightheaded. She looked at the horse standing patiently there, head bent as he sniffed the grass.

'Scared?' asked Greg, mockingly.

'Of you—or the horse? Neither,' she responded pleas-antly, willing herself to calm.

'Then what are we waiting for?'

'What indeed?' she murmured. She looked directly into his eyes, trying to fathom out what was there, what was go-ing on in his head. He was an enigma, and she didn't like men she couldn't understand. She didn't like him anyway, because of who he was, but he would never know that. 'After you,' she added, and watched him mount. He reached down, and she caught his hand and he pulled her up with ease. She was behind him, very close, too close for comfort, and he half turned his head, and she could see the way his hair grew thick and dark, one or two grey threads near his temples, his skin tanned and hard; at least he'd shaved. That was a miracle. She wanted to touch his cheek, to feel the smoothness....

'Put your arms round me,' he said.

'Don't take it personally, will you?' she said in a demure little voice which hid laughter, but Greg didn't answer. He turned away, and Renata slid her arms round him, feeling the hard lean body as her hands reached round and rested on his chest. She was pressing closely to him, her breasts against his back, and she turned her head sideways, and leaned that against him, near his neck, and said: 'I'm ready.'

He clicked his teeth, and the horse began to trot carefully, back in the direction from which they had come. Renata, holding on, was realising some quite disturbing things, one of which was that she was filled with the most incredibly delightful sensation brought on solely by the unavoidable physical contact. This is ridiculous, she thought faintly, but the fact remained. No man had ever had quite this effect on her before. She could feel the hard muscles of his lean body beneath her hands and arms, and she moved slightly, scarcely aware of what she was doing, to ease herself more comfortably into line with him.

The horse made his steady way through the trees, and Greg sat aloof, almost as if she weren't there, not speaking once, guiding the reins, and Renata thought, almost in dismay, that while of course she didn't like him at all, mainly because of who he was, but also because of that brittle arrogance, nevertheless she was finding the ride strangely enjoyable. I'm a masochist, she thought wryly.

He increased speed after they had picked their way through the woods, and they galloped across the grass towards the Towers. Renata clung on, feeling the thrill of speed mingling with the sense of danger—a heady mixture, for the danger wasn't so much physical as the nearness, the touch of body against body; two people who had been crossing swords, metaphorically, since the moment they had first met, and would undoubtedly continue to do so.

Through the wide doors in the wall, the sharp clatter of hooves on cobbles, making her teeth rattle, then she was sliding down, assisted by Greg's strong arm, only he barely turned his head as he helped her, and when she said: 'Thanks for the ride,' he didn't answer, nor did he look at her.

A young man emerged from the stable, accompanied by the dog Toby. He looked at Renata hard, and the dog bounded over to greet her. Greg Masters began to guide the horse into the stable, and the young man followed, after another look, a smile, and a nod at Renata, and as she walked away after patting Toby, she heard Greg's voice, and he seemed to be annoyed.

'I'll find my own way back,' she said to no one in particular, and smiled to herself, gave the dog a final pat, and went over to the door, crossing her fingers that she would actually make it alone.

She did. It was nearly half past eight, and Mrs Masters was walking slowly along towards the sitting room as Renata entered the corridor.

'Good morning, Mrs Masters,' she called.

'Good morning, dear. My, you were up early! Have you been out?'

'Yes. I went to explore the grounds—I hope you don't mind?'

They went in, and Renata helped the old woman to sit down in her favourite seat by the window. 'Mind? Certainly not. Where did you go?'

Renata told her about the hidden valley, and her sur-

prise, and then that Greg had brought her back, and Mrs
Masters listened, and smiled. Renata realised that she was
enjoying the telling of it, that in a way, she was seeing it
through Renata's eyes, and perhaps that was all that she
needed—a new face, a new slant on things. She mentally
decided to dredge out as many anecdotes as she could remember for the older woman, during their morning walks
and talks.

It was during breakfast, after Greg had arrived, and
Christina, a clean-faced Christina dressed in presentable
jeans and smart white tee-shirt, said to her grandmother:
'Please may Renata take me to York this afternoon?' that
things began to get interesting.

'York?' Mrs Masters looked at them both in surprise,
and Greg, who had managed to avoid speaking directly to
Renata, also looked up from his bacon and eggs. 'Well, of
course, dear—but may I ask why?'

Christina gave Renata a silent look of appeal. 'I'm afraid
it was my idea,' Renata said. 'We got talking about books
last night—and found we both have a weakness for bookshops. I was going to mention it to you later this morning,
Mrs Masters, but of course if you have other plans——'

'Not at all. I think the idea is delightful, I was just surprised, that's all.' She smiled gently at her great-granddaughter. 'And I suppose some extra pocket money will be
called for?'

Christina bit her lip. 'Well——' then, seeing the smile
on the old woman's face—'can I, Gran?'

'I'll think about it.' Christina got up and hugged her.

'And how are you planning to go?' Greg asked.

Renata took a careful deep breath. She had done something to annoy him on their ride back. What it was she
couldn't think, but she hadn't imagined his calculated snub
to her in the courtyard, the deliberate turning of his back.
And she hadn't even asked him for a lift. 'I was going to

ask Mrs Masters about that,' she replied calmly, and turned to the older woman with a smile. 'The bus I caught from the station—does that go on to York?'

'I wouldn't hear of you going by bus. George will take you in the car,' said Mrs Masters, and Christina's face fell.

'Can't we, Gran? I'd love to go by bus.'

Mrs Masters laughed. 'Would you, child? It would mean changing—and two hours' journey. You'd hardly have time to browse——'

'Please, Gran!'

'You heard your grandmother,' Greg cut in. 'As a matter of fact I have to go to York today. I can make it this afternoon just as easily. I'll take you both.' He looked at Renata as he said it, but he wasn't smiling, not at all, and she wondered why he had offered if he was as displeased as he looked, but that was his problem, not hers.

'Ah!' Mrs Masters was relieved, you could tell. 'Well then, that settles it.' She beamed at them all.

'Will you come round the bookshops with us, Uncle?' Christina asked.

'I'll see. It depends.'

Depends on what? thought Renata. If you're going to York on business you'll hardly have time. She didn't want him anyway. How could you browse with someone like him standing there? He'd probably disapprove of everything she looked at. He disapproves of *me*, she thought, and that was nearly enough to make her smile, but she refrained, for they would wonder why. She began to mentally calculate how much she could afford to spend. Two paperbacks, no more—or if there were any real secondhand bargains, of course. . . . It was delicious to speculate. That was all part of the fun.

Greg stood up. 'We'll leave immediately after lunch,' he said, looking at his niece. 'See you're ready.'

'We will be.' Her eyes shone. Then he was gone.

'How odd,' the old woman mused. 'He never said anything before—ah well, never mind. You'll travel in comfort.' She smiled at Renata. Odd indeed, Renata thought, and wondered at his reasons. But she didn't guess, not then.... Not until much later.

CHAPTER FIVE

HE's as civilised as civilised can be, thought Renata, as she sat beside Greg in a comfortable seat in a very new Triumph Stag. She had intended sitting in the back with Christina, but after seeing the small place available there, had been obliged to sit in the front. Christina, her legs nearly as long as Renata's, sat cramped happily in the back, talking non-stop to them both.

The morning had passed very pleasantly. Mrs Masters had shown Renata to a secluded garden tucked away at the back of the Towers, out of the public gaze, a high-walled garden with climbing roses and honeysuckle, and a sundial in the centre. Bees droned lazily around searching the flowers for nectar, and the talk of the visitors as they wandered around ebbed and flowed, not near, not far, and there was the slam of car doors, laughter of children from behind the walls, but there they were private, apart from the hubbub, yet in a way enjoying it.

Mrs Masters had brought her tapestry, and asked Renata if she would read to her. She was as keen on books, it seemed, as her great-granddaughter, but found the print of modern ones tiring to her eyes. Renata had agreed happily, slightly startled at the old lady's choice, but wisely saying nothing. She enjoyed nothing so much as a good murder mystery, she confided, and Renata had found a couple of Ruth Rendell's, a choice had been made, and she began to read, and the morning passed with surprising speed.

Now, remembering this in the car as they sped along country roads she turned to Christina. 'It would be a nice idea to buy your grandmother a couple of paperbacks,' she said. 'I was reading a very gory murder to her this morning and she loved it, so I've an idea what to get.'

There was a dry laugh from Greg, a surprised one from Christina. 'Does she?' she asked wide-eyed. '*I* never knew!'

'Get her a dozen or so.' Greg fumbled in his back pocket and handed Renata a twenty-pound note.

'Thank you, I will.' She was startled. She put the note in her purse.

'What about you?' he enquired. 'Do you need any money?'

'No, thanks. I have sufficient.' She had precisely six pounds on her, but she wasn't going to tell him that. And she intended spending no more than two of those, but she wasn't going to tell him that either.

'Only you can have an advance in your salary if you wish,' he said casually.

Renata wondered what it must feel like never to have to bother, never to have to count each pound carefully. It was only a fleeting thought, and she didn't allow herself to dwell on it. 'No, I'm fine,' she said.

His annoyance, or whatever it had been at breakfast, seemed to have faded. He was perfectly polite, but then she knew shrewdly that the presence of his niece had a lot to do with that. The swords were sheathed, temporarily at least.

They were nearing the outskirts of York now, and she asked: 'What time can we have?'

He looked at the dashboard clock, which showed two-thirty just gone.

'How long do you want? It's up to you.'

'But I thought you were going in on business?'

'I am. Only to see someone—it shouldn't take me more than half an hour at most.' He moved his head so as to look at Christina in the driving mirror. 'How would you like me to come round with you, Chris?'

'Would you? Super!' Renata went very still. She couldn't have said why.

'Then I will. I'll drop you near the Minster—I'm not going far away—and meet you at that little café of ours, say,' he frowned, 'three-fifteen? We'll have a cup of coffee then wander round.'

She could go off alone, of course she could. That was clearly what Greg intended. She would wait until they were in the tea-shop, though, and he had met them, and she could wander off and meet them later.

'Smashing! Are you going to treat me?'

'Ah—ah, those who ask ——'

'Don't get,' Christina finished for him, and she was laughing. '*Sorry*, uncle, sorry, I won't ask, honestly.'

'Better not,' but he was smiling.

He slowed down as the traffic grew heavier, weaving a way through until he reached the curb, and there only a few hundred yards away was York Minster, thronged as always with people, tourists from all over the world.

'Out you get. Three-fifteen, don't forget. You know the café?'

'I know it.' Christina leaned over and kissed him on his cheek, and Renata held the door open while Greg held the seat forward for her to scramble out.

They stood on the pavement and watched him drive away and then Renata looked at Christina. 'Now,' she said, 'don't lose me, because *I* don't know where your café is, and I can get lost as easy as pie if I'm deep in a book in a bookshop, okay?'

'Okay,' Christina nodded. 'We'll cross here. The bookshops aren't far away. Come on!' Renata never expected miracles, but a small one certainly seemed to have happened. Christina wore a pretty cotton dress in bright yellow flowered material, and flat sandals, and she had tied her hair back into a ponytail and looked older than fourteen. Renata too had changed from her jeans and wore a very plain blue cotton sun-dress. She tanned easily, and the hours in the garden already showed the effect. She looked stunning, but was scarcely aware of the glances of passing men until Christina tapped her arm and said mischievously: 'Do you know people are looking at you?'

'No.' She stared at the girl. 'Have I got smut on my nose or something?'

'No!' Christina laughed. 'I mean *men* are staring at you. There was one—he nearly fell over.' She giggled, and Renata couldn't help it, she did too.

'Really?' She looked round.

'He's gone now,' Christina whispered. 'He had his camera, and he was just trying to take a photo of the Minster when he saw you and stepped back and nearly fell backwards over the curb. I think he took a photo of you.'

'Did he now? I hope it turns out, then. If he fell over he'd only get the sky, wouldn't he?'

They had crossed the road, and were in a narrow street full of shops of every kind, and people pushed past in every direction, sightseeing, windowshopping, while the sun blazed down from a cloudless sky. It was a glorious day, and it was good to be alive, and be here, now, even if Greg would soon be here as well. She wondered where he had gone, and what business he had that could not be dealt with on the telephone, but she didn't really care because he had got them there, and that was what mattered. Plus the fact that Christina was obviously happy as well. Renata glanced at her as the girl led the way through the crowds. She had no intention of getting lost, but she sensed that it made the girl feel grown up to have a sense of responsibility for her. And Renata intended that they would both enjoy this, their first day together. It was extra important for that reason.

'It would be sensible, Christina,' she said, as they paused outside one of many bookshops, 'if we went to one near this café where we're meeting your uncle, because it's nearly three now so we won't have much time for a look anyway. Then, after we've met him, we can go anywhere we like,' or rather, you can, she added mentally.

'Yes,' the girl nodded. 'It's this way. It's a lovely little place and they do *super* home-made cakes and things.'

'Don't you dare tempt me,' Renata groaned. 'Just a coffee will do me.'

'Wait till you see them! Fresh strawberry tarts with *globs* of cream——'

'Stop!' pleaded Renata, but inwardly she was laughing. She could eat whatever she wanted, whenever she wanted, and never put on an ounce. 'It's all right for you——'

'You've got a super figure.' Christina sighed enviously and looked down at her almost flat chest. 'I wish I had.'

'I'll let you into a little secret, shall I?' They were looking in the window of a dress material shop. 'When I was fourteen I was thinner than you, *and* no bosom *at all*. But I used to do exercises, and play lots of tennis, and go swimming every day—and when I was sixteen——' Renata paused and laughed, and shrugged.

Christina's eyes widened. Slowly she looked up and down, at Renata's voluptuous shape. 'You mean——' she gasped, 'I could——'

'It happened to me. It can happen to you.'

'Gosh!' She peered at her reflection in the shop window. Renata hid her smile. It was working. No need to rush. Time for another surprise.

She pointed casually to a swatch of deep blue material with a silky finish. 'See that?' Christina nodded. 'I could make you a super dress in that if you wanted—something that'd make you look grown up.'

'You could?'

'Yes. I make all my own clothes.'

'Honestly?'

'Yes, honestly,' Renata smiled. 'We'll ask your grand-mother if she'd like me to, shall we? Tell you what, we'll have a look in some dress shop windows, and if you see any you like, I'll copy it.' She patted her bag. 'I always carry a sketch pad and pencil with me and if I see anything *I* want, I draw it, then make.'

'Without a pattern?' Christina was looking at her with something approaching awe now.

'Without a pattern.' Patterns cost money; Renata didn't waste money. She saved it all to pay off her father's debts, but that wasn't for Christina to know.

'Golly, you're *clever*!'

'So are you—don't forget that. Which reminds me, we're going to get some books on German, aren't we?' She looked at a clock suspended over a nearby jeweller's window. 'We'd better go or we'll be late.'

Christina had a lot to think about, and Renata intended to let her. Enough for now anyway. The month's trial had only just begun, but it had begun in the way she intended. If only it wasn't for Greg. . . .

'Here it is. He's waiting!' Christina turned and grinned at Renata, who saw Greg sitting at a table at the back of the long, fairly crowded café. They threaded their way through the tables where people sat drinking tea, and coffee, and cold milk shakes that made your mouth water, and eating cakes that were even more mouthwatering.

Greg stood up. 'This was the only table empty,' he said. 'Just three-fifteen. Well done!' The girls sat down and Christina picked up the menu and began reading it, and Greg looked across at Renata. She couldn't read what was in those dark eyes, but he'd never fall over a curb while gaping at her. He'd never do that. He didn't like her at all.

'I've got such a lot to tell you,' said Christina. 'Renata's going to make me a dress, Uncle, and we've seen some *super* material only she says I've got to ask Gran—and d'you know, she doesn't need a pattern, do you, Renata?—she draws dresses she likes and then makes them! Isn't that super?'

'Super,' he agreed dryly, and his eyes met Renata's again, anl although he was smiling, the smile wasn't for her. The look in his eyes said, clever girl, only he didn't mean it like Christina did, and Renata knew why.

'So can we buy the stuff? 'Cos Gran won't mind—and you can——'

'Hold it,' he said as a waitress came up. 'Let's order. Renata?' Polite, courteous.

'Just coffee, thanks,' she smiled.

'Milk shake—strawberry, please,' Christina looked at the waitress, a girl not much older than herself, 'and three of your special strawberry cakes——'

'Three?' Greg interrupted. 'For *you*?'

'No, one each. I want Renata to try one—please, Uncle.'

'Okay. And coffee for me as well, please.'

'That's two coffees, strawberry shake, three strawberry specials?' The waitress smiled shyly at him, blushing slightly, and went away.

'Please, Renata, just one! You don't mind, do you?'

'No, I don't mind,' Renata laughed. 'In fact I can hardly resist. They look lovely.' She winked at the girl.

'And we're going to learn German, aren't we, Renata? So we're going to buy some books on that—and—what else?' Christina turned to Renata.

'That's about it, I think.' Renata was amused by the girl's enthusiasm. 'Isn't it enough for one day?'

'Yes, I suppose so. Ooh, can we get some tennis balls, Uncle?'

'We've got some.'

'Mmm, I know, but *new* ones. We're going to play, aren't we?'

'Anything *else*?' he enquired dryly.

She was unaware of any sarcasm. 'No, I don't *think* so.'

'Good.' He looked at Renata again. 'So you play well, do you?'

'Well enough. And I enjoy it.' She gave him a pleasant smile. The undercurrents were there, quite suddenly and quite strongly, and Renata spoke gently, as befitted a new employee out for tea with her new employer, because she was ready for any barbs he cared to fire. She'd never met anyone quite like him, admittedly, but she could cope with any man. Any man at all. The fact that he didn't like her only gave the battle an extra edge. 'Do you play tennis?'

'Occasionally. When I have time.'

'I haven't seen the tennis court yet. Perhaps we can have a game later today, Christina?'

'Yes. Got any tennis shoes?'

'I brought mine, yes. They're rather old, but they'll do.' She smiled at the girl warmly.

'Ooh—and a man nearly went *flying* over the curb 'cos he was trying to take a photo of Renata and he stepped back—it was funny, Uncle—you didn't see it, did you, Renata?'

Renata shook her head. Don't make me laugh, she prayed. Greg looked as though he didn't find it funny at all. Christina looked at him, blithely unaware of any atmosphere. 'Lots of men were staring at her——' she sighed. 'Anyway, that's one of the reasons I'm going to play tennis, so's I can have a super figure like her——'

Oh, please, Renata prayed. Please don't let me burst out laughing. His *face*! She dared not look, and glanced round desperately, nails digging into the palm of her right hand.

'Don't you ever stop talking?' said Greg, and Christina looked at him, giggled, and bit her lip.

'Oops. Sorry—it was funny, though.'

'Well, here are our cakes. That might keep you quiet for a second or two—with any luck.' The waitress set the plates out in front of them, Greg paid her, and Renata picked up the tiny cake fork. Rescue at last. She couldn't have lasted more than a few seconds longer.

'Mmm, delicious,' she murmured. It was too. Christina watched her.

'I told you. Mmm, bliss!'

Greg sipped his coffee and watched them eat. 'Want mine?' he asked his niece, and her eyes widened.

'*Can* I? Don't you?'

'I'm not hungry.' He pushed his plate across to her. Now was the moment. Now, while all was well.

'Christina,' said Renata, 'suppose I wander off on my own, now your Uncle Greg's here? You don't mind, do you?' She regarded them both calmly, happily. 'Then if you tell me where we can meet, and what time, I'll be there.'

'But you'll get lost!' The delights of the cakes were suspended for a moment as Christina gazed at Renata anxiously.

'No, I've got a rough idea of where I am now. I'll manage to find my way back to the Minster easily,' Renata assured her. She knew *he* wouldn't mind. In fact he'd probably be relieved. Which only made his response all the more surprising.

'We wouldn't hear of it,' he said calmly. 'Would we, Christina?'

'But really——' Renata felt momentarily confused. Was she hearing correctly?

'But really,' he repeated. 'That would be very bad manners on our part. Together we are, together we stay.' He looked at his watch. 'Eat up, little squirrel, and we'll go.'

Christina obliged, and they wended their way out into the sunshine, Greg leading the way. Two minutes later it became quite clear to Renata that he knew where he was going and was going to decide precisely which shops they went in, and in what order. Her idea of a pleasant lonely browse had vanished. He took them into a large bookshop in an old building in the Shambles and said: 'Right, off you go.'

Christina headed for the section on languages, Renata saw that the book bargains were down a flight of stairs and went down them. She shut Greg out of her mind immediately as the lined shelves came into view. He'd probably blow a little whistle when he decided they'd had enough, she thought, with annoyance. Then she was lost in that other world of books, and he, and Christina, and the Towers, and the reason she was here, all faded into insignificance as she walked slowly along, eyes skimming titles, breathing in the unmistakable scents of old books, the lovely safe perfume of printed pages that was like nothing else in the world.

Time no longer had any importance. It might matter, somewhere in the world outside, but not here. She found a small step ladder seat in a corner, carried her precious pile of books across, and sat down. It was there that Greg found her. She wasn't aware of his approach. She wasn't even aware she was in a bookshop. She was deep in a tattered dog-eared copy of Dodie Smith's *I Capture the Castle*, remembering how it had been the first time she had read it ten years before, reliving it all, when a voice came from nearby: 'Renata?'

She blinked, looked up. Greg stood there. 'Yes?' He crouched down and began looking through the neat stack beside her.

'Are you getting all these?'

'No.' She sighed. 'Where's Christina?'

'Upstairs somewhere buying up the shop. Hmm, what's this? Daphne du Maurier?'

'Yes. It's one I've not read.' She wanted him to go. He was spoiling it. Why didn't he go and leave her alone?

'Why don't you get it, then?'

She looked up at him. They were alone in that shadowy corner. She didn't know what made her say what she did. If she had thought, she wouldn't have, because no one must know, but she didn't have time to think, and she was still in the world of the book she held and the words seemed to come out of their own volition. She regretted them immediately, but it was too late.

'Because I can only afford one here if I want to buy anything else,' she said. 'Because I'm allowing myself two pounds——'

'Two? You won't get much for that,' he said, amused. The glint of laughter in his eyes did it. What did he know? He never had to *think* about money.

'Precisely,' she snapped. 'Which is why I'm choosing carefully.'

'And these others?' he tapped the stack. 'All books you'd like?'

'Perhaps. Why don't you leave me alone?'

'You said you had enough when I offered you an advance on——'

'Two pounds is enough. For me. It sharpens the mind wonderfully, poverty does. You should try it some time.' She could hear the words coming out. She wanted to stop them, but she couldn't. 'It's not a question of an advance, it's a question of how much I can allow myself to spend—and you sure as heck wouldn't understand that, would you?' She stood up and faced him. 'I save all my money—*all* of it, except the merest bit for luxuries like books—and if you want to go, why don't you? You can leave me here'—she wanted to stop, but the words kept pouring out, and she listened aghast to herself, as if it were someone else talking, 'and collect me later——'

'Why?'

'Why what? Why do I want to be left here? It's obvious,

isn't it?' she said breathlessly. His face was shadowed, dark, and he was probably very angry, but the laughter, the *scorn*, when she had said two pounds, had been more than enough for her.

'Why do you save all your money?' His voice was hard, and she thought how she hated him at that moment.

'That's none of your business.' Their voices were quiet, both of them, and yet the intensity was there, and it was the swords again, clashing. The tension simmered around them in that small corner, and no one else in the basement fortunately, for the atmosphere was electric enough to shock anyone approaching. She wanted to hurt him, to scream, and to hit him, to lash out, and she felt faint at the thought because no one could affect her like that, only he did. She saw his face change when she told him it was none of his business, saw a deep, deep anger on his face and in his eyes, and she wondered if he wanted to strike her, and what she would do if he did. Then she heard his indrawn breath——

'None of my business?' he shot back, the words rapier-sharp. 'But I think it is.'

'Why?' She lifted her chin and stared into the dark eyes, seeking she knew not what.

'Because I am employing you——'

'Correction. Your grandmother is.'

'Correction. *I* am.' Whispering steel, the words harder than steel. 'And do I pay you so poorly that you must save every penny?'

'No.' His words had stunned her. Not Mrs Masters, but *him*. She was answerable to him. 'No,' she repeated. 'But I must——'

'Is that why you wear no make-up? Make all your own clothes?'

'Is that anything to do with you? Do you doubt my honesty? Is that it? Are you frightened I might be tempted——'

'No. But I wonder about you——'

'Then don't. I am honest. I take nothing from anyone.' She was trembling, shaking with anger and fear of him, and she had never done that before, but he made her feel weak and helpless, and she didn't like it but there was nothing she could do about it. 'Let me be. Leave me!' Her voice broke as she fought to control threatening tears. She never cried——

'That is not what I meant.' His voice had gone harsh.

'Then what? What do you mean?'

Christina clattered down the stairs. '*There* you are!' she said. 'I wondered——' she stopped. It was as if something of the tension surrounding them had hit her suddenly. Renata turned. The spell was broken. She was still shaking, but she began to breathe deeply, fighting for calm. Christina walked more slowly down the last few steps, as if apprehensive. She carried a plastic shopping bag that bulged with books.

Renata gave her a shaky smile. 'Your uncle said you were buying up the shop,' she said. 'I can see he was right.' Greg had turned round.

'Good grief,' he said. 'How many have you bought?' His voice was calm, tightly controlled. Renata knew that as surely as she knew about herself. The jagged edges of his anger still touched her raw nerves, and she knew with a deep certainty that there was more to come. But not here, not now, not—yet.

'Ooh, I don't know!' Christina jumped the last step. 'Lots and lots. What are you getting, Renata?'

'There's one here you'd like,' Renata handed her the Dodie Smith book. 'Have you read it?'

Christina took it. 'No,' she said. 'Is it good?'

'Yes. You'll like it. I'm going to buy it because I don't have a copy, but I'll lend it to you first.'

'Thanks.'

Greg picked up the precious stack from the floor and walked towards the stairs. 'Oh, wait,' Renata exclaimed. 'I must put them back ——'

He turned. 'Too late. I've been looking for these for ages.' He went up. Christina held up the book Renata had handed to her, and giggled.

'Come on, he'll get this as well if we're quick!' She scampered up after him. Renata remained where she was. She had gone cold. She didn't know what his motives were in taking the books, but she didn't like it. She walked slowly up the stairs; he was paying, and the books were being put into a bag.

'What's the matter?' Christina left him and walked over to Renata.

She gave herself a mental shake. 'Nothing.' She managed to smile. 'Do you know, I lost all count of time down there. It's—good heavens—it's nearly half past four!'

'Never mind. Time for a quick look somewhere else.' They walked out, Greg behind them, carrying the bag.

'I mustn't forget to buy the books for your grandmother,' Renata said to Christina as they strolled along in the sun, mingling with the ever-present tourists and holidaymakers who thronged the pedestrian walkway. No traffic was allowed in the street, so there was no danger from cars. They went in another bookshop, and there Renata found, and bought, ten paperbacks that she felt sure Mrs Masters would enjoy, and then, as they came out, Greg said to his niece:

'Okay. Where's the shop with your material?'

'Can we?' She held his arm tightly. 'Down here, this way——' She pulled him along, as though he might change his mind if he had time to think about it. 'Not far now——'

Renata followed, walking more slowly, keeping them in sight. Greg carried her books, *her* books, the ones she had chosen, in a bag. He had bought them. It seemed an intrusion of privacy. When they reached the dress material shop, and stopped, waiting for her, she handed Greg the six pounds change from his twenty-pound note. He looked at it as he took it, and she said softly, so that Christina, busily peering in the window, wouldn't hear:

'It's quite correct. I'll show you what I bought. The prices are on.' He turned away without a word.

'Right, in you go. Is that it?' he said. 'Looks nice.' He turned to Renata. 'Get what you want.'

'Three yards should do it.' He was angry, but no more so than she. The air crackled with the electricity. She hated him; he hated her. And that was that.

She went in, they bought the material and matching cotton, and came out again. 'Time to go home,' he said. 'We don't want to get caught in the traffic. This way.'

He strode off, and they followed. 'It's been a super afternoon,' said Christina. 'Have you enjoyed it, Renata?'

'Yes, very much.' She smiled down at her, and saw the girl's face change suddenly. Renata looked in the direction Christina's eyes were fixed, looked back at her, saw them widen, saw the sudden twist of her mouth. 'Christina?' she said. 'What——'

'It's *her*,' the girl whispered.

Well ahead of them, walking towards them, came a man, a woman, and an Afghan hound. The three made an elegant tableau, and it seemed as if others appreciated this, for the people moved aside for them as though they were royalty. And Renata knew.

They had seen Greg, who was walking ahead of them. The next few moments were to remain etched in Renata's mind for quite a while, so vivid were they. The woman paused. To Renata's not quite objective eyes, it seemed a dramatic, theatrical pause. 'Darling!' she cried. Greg, being several yards ahead of Renata and Christina, appeared to be alone. And something made Renata catch the girl's arm, so that she had to pause.

'Who is it, Christina?' she asked innocently.

Equally innocent eyes turned to her. 'Oh, Virginia, Uncle Greg's girl-friend.' The flash of recognition in which Renata had seen dismay—or possibly dislike—had gone. Christina's face was expressionless.

'I see,' Renata smiled pleasantly. 'They'll want to talk for a moment, I suppose. What a lovely dog that is. Is it hers?'

'Mmm.' The man and woman now stood with Greg, who hadn't yet looked back to see where they were. Perhaps he's forgotten us, thought Renata hopefully, and half turned so that she was looking in a sweetshop window. It was quite natural to do so, they had been close to it anyway. So that's the lovely Virginia, she thought, watching her reflection in the window. 'Can I go and get some sweets for Gran, Renata?'

'Of course. What a nice idea. Got enough money?'

'Yes.' Christina vanished inside the crowded shop, Renata continued to look in the window as if fascinated by its array of goodies, but she was watching her employer, his girl-friend, and the man. Who was he? Tall, well built, dark tanned, about thirty, he was smoothly good-looking. Virginia was elegant, dark-haired and extremely attractive. Renata admitted that to herself without being aware of the tiny pang that assailed her. Virginia wore a brilliant blue silky tunic and tight white trousers and spiky, tottery high-heeled sandals. She was extremely slender. Some women might have said she was skinny, but Renata, who had never been jealous of another woman in her life, thought her very slim and elegant.

And then Greg turned. He's looking for us, she thought, and waited, shifting her eyes so that he wouldn't see her looking at his reflection. She waited very calmly for him to come over and find her. Christina was nowhere near being served. She would be inside there for several minutes more. Then he was beside her. 'Where's Christina?' he asked.

'In there getting something for Mrs Masters.' She was able to turn, to look, to see, beyond him, the couple waiting with the Afghan.

'Come over and meet some friends,' he said.

'All right.' She turned away from the window and walked back with him to where Virginia and the man stood talking, as though totally uninterested in where Greg had gone. But Virginia was watching her, and Renata knew that cool assessing look of old. She had seen it too many times in other women's eyes. And suddenly, for some obscure reason, it made her feel quite pleased.

CHAPTER SIX

IT wasn't easy, it really wasn't easy, Renata found, to remain pleasant. But she managed. For Virginia's eyes, although beautiful, a deep blue, almost violet, and thickly lashed, were cold and hard as they shook hands, and the dislike that hit Renata like a tangible force would have felled a lesser woman. Renata, well used to it, could not only cope, but found it yet another challenge. She was not as elegant as Virginia but she had advantages that more than balanced the other's undeniable sophistication.

'How do you do,' she said, and smiled warmly at them both. The man, Ian Mannering, was Virginia's cousin. He was pleasant enough, no dislike there, but an equally warm smile, and a handshake that lasted a fraction too long.

'And you say Renata's looking after both your grandmother and Christina?' Virginia said to Greg, as if continuing a conversation. She turned to Renata again. 'How *nice* for you. The Towers is a beautiful place to be in summer.'

'It is. I've only been there since yesterday, so I've not seen all round, but I'm sure I'm going to be happy working there.'

'I'm sure.' Her eyes raked Renata's face. She was angry, but Renata would have taken a bet that neither man was aware of it.

'Have you always done *this* kind of work?' she asked. Putting me in my place, thought Renata. And nicely too. The girl-friend showing interest in the staff. She wondered what the reaction would be if she bobbed a little curtsey and the thought made her smile.

'No,' she answered, and that was all.

'Visiting long, Ian?' asked Greg.

'Just a few days. Then I'm off to the States for a couple of weeks.' Ian grinned at Renata. 'We're having a party on Friday,' he turned to Virginia. 'Why don't we invite Renata, Ginny?'

If looks could kill, you'd be dead, thought Renata. Dear me, how would Virginia get out of that one?

'That's a kind thought.' Greg said it, almost as if amused.

'How nice of you to ask,' Renata looked at Virginia, as though *she* and not her cousin had issued the invitation, 'but I'm afraid I've nothing to wear——'

'Come as you are!' Ian seemed to be taking it the invitation had been confirmed.

'Oh, darling!' Virginia batted long eyelashes at him. 'You heard Renata. That's always a tactful way of saying one doesn't want to come—after all, you won't know anybody, will you?' She gave Renata a lovely warm all-girls-together, and we-understand smile.

'But thank you for asking me. Oh, I'd better go and find Christina. She'll be wondering where we are, excuse me, won't you?' Renata smiled, turned away, and walked slowly towards the shop. The lovely Virginia certainly was lovely —on the surface. What she was like underneath Renata didn't fancy to hazard a guess. She and Greg were well suited. She went in to find Christina, who was just being served.

It was a pleasant evening, and it was natural for them to play tennis, after dinner when Mrs Masters was settled by the television with a good programme to watch, and Greg had vanished somewhere. He had bought two boxes of tennis balls after they had left Virginia and her cousin, and not a word more had been said about the party.

James Harlow had telephoned while they were dining,

and Renata rang him back afterwards. True to the promise he had made Renata, he was keeping an eye on Neil, and he wanted to know if he could come up to see Renata that weekend. She managed to get out of it by telling him— quite truthfully—that as she was still very new, and settling in, it might be better if he left it until the following week. He'd phone again, he told her, and was missing her.

She had hung up, vaguely uneasy, knowing she would never miss him, certainly never love him. She wished he didn't love her. She wanted him as a friend, no more. He was steady and dependable, but never in a million years would he arouse that spark in her that she knew was essential for marriage or any deep relationship.

She was glad of the chance of physical exercise. The parcel from Diana hadn't yet arrived—no great surprise that. Mrs Masters had assured her that any post always took a day or so extra in their rural backwater. There was no rush. She had only been at Falcon Towers just over twenty-four hours. Sometimes, it seemed as if she had always been there....

'This way, Renata.' Christina had changed into white shorts and top. She led her down the stairs, along passages —Renata was already lost—and past a courtyard that looked vaguely familiar, out into a shady tree-lined tennis court. The net was hanging limply from the supports, and a few dead leaves lay forlornly on the red shale. It was a nice court, and Renata looked round appreciatively. They were hidden from the main building, totally surrounded, outside the wire fencing, by trees. There was a long bench at one side, and on there they changed their shoes and left the spare balls and racquet covers.

'I hope you're good,' said Renata, as she tied her laces.

Christina giggled. 'Not very. But you're going to teach me, aren't you?'

'I'm going to try.' She looked up at the girl, who stood

impatiently dancing from one foot to the other, waiting for her. 'Well? How's it going?'

'How's what going?' Christina looked vaguely puzzled.

'I've been here a full day. We've had a few talks, played a couple of games, been on a trip to bookshops, and now we're going to play tennis. There's another twenty-seven days to go of my "trial" month. Think we'll both stick it?'

Christina grinned and sat down on the bench. Then the grin disappeared. 'I was a pig, wasn't I?'

'A bit,' Renata grinned back.

'But you're different—you're not stuffy like the others. I guess I needed someone to tell me.' She smiled slightly. 'And you did—and you know something? I suddenly knew you were right. I—like you, Renata.' She went pink. 'Gosh, I'm sorry—that was a bit sloppy, wasn't it?'

'No,' said Renata levelly. 'I like you. Okay? Tennis now? Let's see how good—or bad—you are. You may teach *me* a thing or two.' She picked up two balls. 'We'll have a knockabout first, see how we go.'

The next half hour they both concentrated. It took Renata only minutes to see that Christina had the potential to be a good player, but was lazy. She reacted accordingly, telling the girl to move, showing her how to gauge distance and bounce, playing gently, allowing her to expand her movements until she began to really enjoy the game.

They stopped for a breather and Christina produced a flask of orange juice from her bag, and they sipped slowly, discussing various points of the game they had just played. Christina learnt quickly. This was something Renata was beginning to appreciate. She felt like a teacher, and she felt the joy a good teacher must feel on seeing a pupil begin to truly learn, and enjoy.

They played five games more, and Christina was moving quickly now, having the natural advantage of younger limbs and abundant energy, which Renata suspected hadn't been fully used. They finished a hard-fought game, a narrow win for Christina after several deuces, and Renata cried: 'Enough! I need a sit-down. Any more orange juice?' Christina skipped over to the bench, laughing.

'*This* is going to give me a super figure?' she said, laughing.

'If I live long enough,' Renata groaned, rubbing her ankle. 'Phew, give me a minute!'

'Okay.' Christina sat down and handed Renata the flask cup. 'Oh, here's Uncle Greg.'

Renata looked up to see him striding out of the trees towards them. She watched him. Now that she knew he was her employer, she wondered if he had come to see if she was earning her money. 'So it is,' she said mildly. Let him say anything. This was evening, and it was *he* who had reminded her that she didn't have to work all the time. 'Why don't you have a game with him, and I'll watch?' she suggested.

No sooner said than done. Christina jumped up. 'Hey, Uncle,' she called. 'Want a game?'

He was crossing the court now. 'I'll thrash you,' he said, and grinned at her.

'Yes, you probably will, but never mind.' She handed him the racquet that Renata had been using. 'Come on!'

Renata watched them, and thought about the party invitation for the following night. His world, and Virginia's world, was no longer hers, but the subtle implication of Virginia's, that she would be out of her depth, still lingered. She hadn't wanted Renata, and she had made it obvious. Renata smiled to herself. I wonder why? she thought. And I wonder why he's come out here? She watched the play, contented to sit there, happy to see the girl who, only yesterday, had resented her coming, so clearly enjoying herself. The score was immaterial. Whether Greg allowed her to win or not didn't matter. It was a pleasant evening, cool after a hot day, with the sun turning the leaves on the trees to soft gold, and a slight breeze making them shiver and shimmer.

'Oh damn! That wasn't *fair* — it was just in!' Christina wailed. 'Renata, wasn't that in?'

'Yes,' said Renata promptly, even though she hadn't been watching, not properly anyway.

'All right, minx, your point. Deuce again.' Greg glared at Renata. 'Women!' he added, as he strode back to serve again. Renata laughed. She found it funny.

The game was over moments later, and Greg, naturally, had won. he turned to Renata. 'All right,' he said, 'let's see how well you do, shall we?'

She looked at him. 'You want a game with *me*?'

'That is what I was asking, yes,' he responded with gentle irony.

'Go on, Renata, you *show* him! She's *good*,' Christina said accusingly to Greg.

He raised an eyebrow, amused. 'I believe you, Chris. I am also aware if there's any doubt about a point, that judgment will go against me. However,' he paused, 'I think I'll cope.'

Renata stood up slowly and had a little stretch. She was looking forward to this. She hadn't even contemplated a game with him when he had appeared. She hadn't extended herself with Christina, merely played an average game, because that had been enough for the child to cope with. But Greg was different, oh, very different. For an obvious start, he was a man, and had the natural advantage of greater muscular power. He had played Christina at her own level, as he should. But there was this other thing, that no one knew about, the hidden, secret thing between them, stretched as taut as gauze, and as shimmery and amorphous. There was the brittle tension that enwrapped them, the subtle challenge, the fire of battle.

She wasn't really tired. She hadn't been, before. It had

been nice to pretend so, to have a rest. But now, suddenly, she was alive, tingling and ready for action, all senses attuned. She was ready for him. And she was determined to beat him.

'Best of five?' she said, gently, carelessly, as though it didn't matter.

'Have you got that much energy?' He was amused, patronising, the strong dominant male.

'Well, I'll do my best,' she said modestly.

'I'll be umpire,' said Christina, and perched herself on the bench, bottom on back, feet on seat, voice important.

Greg groaned, 'That's all I need!' It was a game—an amusement, no more. But it wasn't, and they both knew it. On one level it was for Christina, on another, it was part of the battle.

He threw a coin for server, and Renata won, then they were away. She took a deep breath as she went to the baseline to serve, and smiled to herself. She didn't care how good he was—and he probably would be—she was going to win.

They were level, two all, and stopped for a breath before the final game, when Greg looked at Renata and said, almost accusingly: 'You're a damned good player.'

'So are you.' She ached in every inch of her. Her muscles cried out—enough! and she dared not sit down, lest she find herself unable to get up ever again, so she stood there, trying to look casual. Christina was hugging her knees, unable to bear the tension, muttering: 'Gosh!' from time to time, staring wide-eyed at them both, and Renata knew what she meant. It had been—still was—a battle of epic proportions, no quarter given, every point fought for, superb play on both sides. Greg was a ruthless player, but Renata had the advantage of years of practice combined with lightning reflexes.

'Ready, partner?' he said, tone faintly mocking.

'Ready.' She wanted to crawl away and die, but she walked carefully, quietly, to her side. It was her service. And this was it—the final game. She put everything she had into that first service. It slammed across the court, left him standing. An ace. Her point. She laughed inwardly. She was going to win, she knew it now. She was going to beat him and wipe that mocking smile from his face.

Then, at deuce, she ran for a devilish return which came low and straight, hit it, turned to move back, anticipating his shot—and her leg twisted and she stumbled. She was up in a moment, but the sky spun round crazily, and she felt a pounding in her head, a throbbing pain, drumming her ears, turning, twisting— Pain filled her, and it seemed that a hum grew louder, and vibrated in her ears—and the ground seemed to be coming up to meet her. Renata put her hands over her ears to shut out the sound, and the next moment she was caught and held in a pair of very power- ful arms.

'Stay still,' the voice said, and it was Greg's. He lifted her and carried her to the bench, and sat her down, and she was aware that Christina watched her, white-faced, anxious, but for the moment she couldn't do anything to reassure her, although she wanted to.

'My leg——' she said faintly. 'I twisted it——'

'Don't try to talk.' His voice was reassuring, safe. 'It's all right. It's my fault——'

'It's not,' she whispered fiercely. 'I turned badly.' She was recovering rapidly, the world coming into focus again. 'It'll be all right in a moment, honestly.'

'We'll call it a draw. That's an order. There is no way I'm going to finish that game tonight. Can you walk?'

'Yes, I think so.'

'Christina, get the racquets, love, and Renata's shoes. I'll help her back to the house.'

'Yes, Uncle.'

Greg took over, without seeming to, almost casually, and minutes later he was walking Renata back to the house. She was feeling better, well enough to wonder what the lovely Virginia would say if she should arrive at that moment. Greg had his arm around Renata, round her waist, and he paced his steps to hers, so that they walked in step, slowly. Christina had run on ahead; he had told her to.

'Really, I'm fine. I slipped, was jolted—but all's well.'

'You never give up, do you?' he asked. 'I mean, *never* give up.'

'I don't know what you mean,' she retorted.

'Don't you?' He slowed his step, looked down at her. 'You should do.'

She decided to ignore the subtle undertones. 'It's making a big fuss about nothing. Look, see—I can walk unaided,' and she pulled away from him and walked, a little slowly, but perfectly steadily. 'See? A twisted muscle, no more. Tomorrow it will be as though it never happened.'

'So you'll be fit for the party?'

'Yes—*if* I were going.'

'And you're not?' He opened the gate for her and they went in.

'No. I thought that was decided.' She winced with pain, and he caught her arm.

'Steady,' he warned.

'It was nothing. Thank you.' She gently disengaged her arm.

'Why don't you want to go? Was it because you had nothing to wear? I thought that was one of those corny excuses women use when they've a wardrobe full of clothes.'

'But in my case it happens to be true. I don't. You saw my case. How many wardrobefuls do you think that contained?' She smiled, paused to let him open a door to inside. 'And anyway, I'm not a partygoer. I don't drink, or

smoke, or wear make-up—as you remarked only recently——'

'That was an unpardonable and personal remark.'

'Nevertheless it was true. I don't.' She laughed. 'Your
friend Miss Mannering did the right thing in pointing out
that I'd be out of place. I would.'

They were climbing stairs now, he beside her, both
walking slowly. The tension, never far away, washed around
them now that they were alone, and it was a breathless,
tangible force she couldn't deny or pretend wasn't there,
because it was, and she hoped that he wouldn't say more,
because she'd put the party out of her mind. She didn't
want to think or talk about it. She wouldn't go anywhere
she wasn't wanted. It was Virginia's party, and Virginia
definitely didn't want her, and Renata, who didn't like
parties anyway, would much prefer to read a good book or
curl up on a comfortable chair to watch television. But she
was sure Greg wouldn't understand that. He and Virginia
were two of a kind, birds of a feather.

He touched her arm when she stumbled slightly; the
touch was an electric shock up her arm, brief but powerful,
and she noticed that he took his hand away instantly.

'I'll—go to my room, and wash,' she said, feeling her
heart quicken.

'Yes, of course.'

They came up the main staircase, and she expected him
to go to the lounge, but he walked the side corridor with
her instead. She opened her door and paused.

'Thank you for the game—even though it wasn't
finished,' she said. 'Perhaps, another day——'

'Yes.' He pushed the door wider. 'Try not to fall asleep
with your light on again, won't you?'

She stared at him, stunned. 'Had I——'

'You had. When I came to bed, about three, the light
was showing under your door.'

Renata tried to stem the warm tide of colour flooding her face, and Greg added, quite gently for him: 'I knocked quietly, but there was no answer. In case you were ill I opened the door carefully and looked in. You were fast asleep with three magazines in imminent danger of falling to the floor with resounding thuds——' he smiled. 'I removed them, and switched off the light. I promise you, you never stirred.'

'I wondered, when I woke—then I forgot. Thank you.' She turned away. This was enough. She was disturbed, uneasy, though she didn't know why, but if he talked much longer she might give herself away, her precious self-confidence no longer giving her the weapons to deal with him. . . .

'Be careful. You'll go into the lounge when you're ready? My grandmother enjoys her coffee and biscuits before she goes to bed, and she likes company.'

'Of course. I'll only be a few minutes.' She closed the door gently after he walked away. Her leg was all right now. Had she been playing with anyone else, she would have rested for a few minutes and then forgotten about it, but with Greg—she thought about it, remembering, as she washed her hands and face. Remembering the strength of him as he had lifted her—and something else. Almost a concern. Which was ridiculous. The sharp tap at the door brought her out of her introspection. It was Christina, with her sandals. 'Oh, come in.' Renata was drying her hands and face. 'If you wait a moment I'll walk with you to the lounge.'

'Are you all right?' The girl's face was anxious.

'Yes, thanks, I'm fine now. That was a silly thing for me to do—and *me* trying to show *you* how to play!' She laughed. 'Never mind, we'll play again tomorrow, or perhaps go swimming.'

'I'm going to ask Uncle Greg to get me a bike.'

Renata laughed. 'Don't push your luck! New tennis balls, material for a dress, books—he'll wonder what I'm getting you into!'

'No, he won't. He doesn't mind, honestly. He said——' Christina stopped abruptly.

Renata's curiosity was aroused. 'Yes? Said what?' she asked—very casually.

'Oh, nothing—it wasn't to me,' Christina muttered. 'I mean, I just happened to hear him talking to Gran, and——'

'Oh, I see. Well, as it wasn't meant for you, perhaps you'd better not tell me,' said Renata gently. 'Now, I'm ready. Are you coming to the lounge?' She would have *loved* to know. . . .

'Yes. Hey, we forgot to talk French, didn't we?'

'Ah, oui, c'est vrai, mais il n'est pas trop tard. Bien! Dis quelque chose en français pour moi, mon enfant.'

Christina giggled. 'Gosh, that's good! Okay, here goes——' and she launched into a discussion on the events of the day, walking slowly out of Renata's room as she spoke, and Renata answered. The girl's accent was very schoolgirl French, but her grasp of words was good, and she understood everything Renata said. They lingered in the hall near the staircase as the French words rattled back and forth and time was forgotten. Until they heard the lounge door opening and looked guiltily round to see Greg walking towards them. Christina's words tailed away.

'Oh. We were talking French,' she said.

'So I gathered,' he said dryly. 'I could hear you down there. Your poor grandmother thinks you've both got lost. So, if you don't want a telling off in French, you'd better get moving.'

'Hah, bet you couldn't,' Christina said cheekily as they walked towards him. She ducked the hand that shot out to slap her bottom, and ran into the lounge. Renata followed at more sedate pace. Mrs Masters was watching the television. Her eyes lit up as they came in.

'Now, how did the tennis go?' she asked, patting the settee beside her for Christina to sit down. Greg hadn't followed them in. Renata sat down on an overstuffed easy chair that was blissfully comfortable, and prepared to listen. There was a coffee pot, and cups, on a tray set near the old woman, and a plateful of chocolate biscuits. It was nearly ten o'clock, still light outside, with a faintly pink light coming through the windows. The atmosphere was one of peace.

'And how is your leg now, my dear?' Mrs Masters' voice roused Renata from a quiet drifting of thought.

'Oh, fine, really. It was nothing at all.'

'Then it won't stop you going to the party? That's good.'

Renata looked at her, startled. Greg must have told her. But why? 'Oh no, I wasn't going anyway,' she answered.

'Heavens, why not, child?'

Because Virginia didn't invite me, her cousin did, and he should have known better—but she couldn't say that. 'Well, I'm not a party person, I suppose.' Renata gave a demure smile.

'Oh. Greg seemed to give me the impression you had no "party" clothes——'

'Ah, well, that too——'

'But my dear, I told you, I've got those lovely Fortuni dresses you *must* try on.'

'Oh, it's very kind of you, but——' how did she get out of that? She swallowed. 'I don't know anyone.' That seemed feeble, even to Renata's own ears, but it was the best she could do. She was confused as to why Greg should have bothered to tell his grandmother. As if it were *important*.

'You know Greg—you've met Virginia, such a *kind* girl —and her cousin Ian. Greg seemed to think he was quite taken with you.'

'He was very—pleasant,' Renata agreed. Help! she added inwardly.

'Wish I'd been invited. It's not fair, being fourteen,' said Christina, effectively coming to the rescue. Both women laughed, and her grandmother said kindly:

'You'll be old enough soon.'

'Hmm, everyone tells me that.' She grinned at Renata. 'If you go, you can tell me everything that happens. That'll be nearly as good as going, specially if you tell me in French!'

'There's a thought,' agreed Renata. 'Homework without tears.'

'So will you go?'

She shook her head gently. 'I don't think so. Really, I'd much prefer to stay at home and read a book.'

'That's nice,' Mrs Masters beamed. 'You called this home—I hope that's how you feel.'

Renata looked at her. 'So I did. Yes, I do, I hope that doesn't sound presumptuous of me——'

'Not at all. But you should go. You're young, you're at the age when you should be out enjoying yourself. Life isn't all work, my dear, and I'd be the first to tell you that I don't want you to feel tied down here. Your weekends are your own, you know, and your evenings.'

'You're very kind.' They looked up as the door opened, and Greg came in.

Christina jumped up to pour out the coffee, and Mrs Masters looked at her grandson.

'We're having a hard job persuading Renata to go to Virginia's party tomorrow—and I'm sure my Fortuni dresses would fit her. I do wish you'd try on one, my dear. Christina, you know where they are, don't you? Take Renata now—the coffee will keep—and show her.' She smiled at Renata. 'Do me the favour of trying one on and come in and show me. Will you?'

Christina handed her grandmother a cup of coffee. 'Come on, Renata!'

It was three against one. As Renata stood up, she wondered why. The old woman, and Christina she could understand, but not Greg. He stood by the door and looked at her. He didn't smile; his face was quite expressionless. He merely stood there, his eyes upon her, and she couldn't see what was going on in his mind. He was like a hawk, dark, watchful, almost sinister.

They went out, along, down stairs, into a labyrinth of passages and doors, so confusing. Christina opened a door and peeped in. 'Here we are.' She switched on the light, for the room had no windows, only long mirrors. It was like a huge changing room, long glass-doored wardrobes lined two walls, and there was an old chest of drawers to which she went. She opened a drawer and drew out what looked like a twisted skein of thread, then she shook it out. Renata gasped, she couldn't help it. Christina was holding up a dress. It was the dress every woman dreamed of possessing —a floating dream, a poem in itself, shimmering silk in gold that shaded to russet, finely pleated, the lines flowing but so simple, swirling as Christina moved it. Renata went forward to touch it.

'It's gorgeous,' she whispered. She lifted the skirt of the dress to one side, and the fine silk whispered, and the movement of it was liquid. Like molten gold, she thought, pure molten gold. There was a pattern, an abstract pattern in deeper or lighter shades of russet and gold; the neckline was softly scooped, the sleeves floating away....

'You win,' she grinned weakly at the girl. There was no way she was going to allow this to be put away without trying on.

'There's several more. Look!' Renata peeped into the open drawer. It was a treasure trove of greens, blues, reds, all lying twisted and skein-like.

'I don't believe it.' She held the dress up. 'I'll put it on now. Just this one.' She knew it would fit. She was very tall, and it would probably come mid-calf, but that was the fashionable length now. Renata slipped off her dress and handed it to Christina, then put on the dress very carefully, slowly—and looked in the mirror.

'Gosh, it's *super*!' breathed Christina. 'It's like it was made for you! Oh, Renata, it's absolutely *super*!'

Renata turned, quickly, pirouetting round, swirling the full skirt, which was, as she had thought, mid-calf length, and when she stopped moving the material settled, clinging, finely pleated, softly outlining her figure.

She almost wished she was going to the party—and dismissed the thought immediately. 'It is lovely,' she agreed. 'And it feels good to wear—let's go and show your grandmother, shall we?'

'Hey, what about shoes?' Christina looked at Renata's flat sandals, and frowned slightly. 'I mean—um—they don't *quite* go——'

Renata laughed. 'I know what you mean.' She slipped them off. 'That better for you, madam?'

'There are some here, on shoe trees. My gran's old ones.'

'Oh, but no, they wouldn't fit——'

'Sh!' said Christina. She pushed back a heavy glass door. 'Come over here. What size are you?'

'Six—but——' Renata followed her over to see rows of shoes on racks. Surely the old lady wouldn't wear a size six? But she did. Christina produced a pair triumphantly. They were black satin, high-heeled, with long pointed toes, and straps, and a diamanté buckle. Extremely old-fashioned, but perfect for the dress. Renata, bemused, slipped them on. They not only fitted, but were surprisingly comfortable. She looked down at them, standing like a model, toes out, slim ankles showing to their best. 'Golly,' she said.

'Golly yes,' Christina echoed. 'You must go. *Please* go. You'll knock Virginia's eyes out.' She giggled and put her hand to her mouth. 'Oops—sorry! I shouldn't have said that.'

'No, you shouldn't,' answered Renata severely. 'I'll pretend you didn't.'

'I don't like her.'

'I gathered that.'

The girl's eyes widened. 'How? I never said——'

'I saw your face, today, when *you* saw *her*.' Renata smiled. 'We can't like everybody, you know. But it's important not to let it show.' And heaven help me, she thought. Who am I to lecture her on manners when it's all I can do to prevent myself hitting her uncle nearly every time we meet?

'I don't. She's always buying me presents anyway. 'Cos she's mad about Uncle Greg——'

'Christina love, I don't think you ought to be telling me this.'

'There's no one else I *can* tell,' the girl answered logically enough. 'Gran sort of likes her, and Uncle Greg's potty about her——'

'I'm sure she's very nice,' Renata said hastily. 'And she's got a lovely dog——'

'Huh! That's her mother's. *She's* all right, but Virginia just likes to parade round with poor old Charley.'

'Charley?' Renata burst out.

'Charles Algernon Fitzwalter the second,' giggled Christina. 'That's a mouthful, isn't it? He's stupid, like her. All *she* thinks about is how gorgeous she looks——'

'Well, she did. That outfit she had on today was super. And she's very slim—a bit your build, in fact. Bet you'd look nice in a tunic like she had on——' They both looked at each other as the same thought struck them.

'Would you——' said Christina at the same moment that Renata said:

'Should I——' They both burst out laughing.

'Snap!' Renata answered. 'Want me to make you an outfit like that?'

'Could you?'

'I don't see why not. Let's go back and show your grand-mother this dress, and tomorrow we'll discuss the matter.'

They went out, leaving Renata's dress and sandals in the room, and made the tortuous way back. Christina led the way as they neared the lounge, and held out her arm. 'Wait,' she said importantly. 'I'll announce you. Gran will like that.'

She flung wide the door. 'Miss Renata Page,' she intoned in ringing voice. Renata walked in. She had imagined that Greg would have gone and Mrs Masters would be alone, but he was there, standing by the window looking out. And as she went in, he turned slowly round. He turned, and looked across the room at her, and it was very strange, but it was as if, for a few moments, no one else was there. She saw only him, his eyes, dark and shadowed, for the light was behind him, and it was as if, for an electric moment in time, neither could look away from the other. The spell was broken by the old lady's voice.

'Oh, Renata my dear, how lovely you look!' She held out her hand. 'Come over here where I can see you properly.' Slowly, Renata walked towards her. She felt as if she were floating. The dress swirled round her with each movement, and she walked straight and tall, almost gliding across the carpet, feeling lightheaded, as if indeed she might well float away. . . .

'Oh yes. Ah, the memories this brings back!' The old lady shook her head. 'I never imagined I would see this dress worn again——' she turned to Greg. 'Doesn't she look lovely, Greg?'

'Indeed she does, Grandmother.' But his voice was ex-pressionless. Only his eyes said what his lips did not, but Renata couldn't read what they were saying. She twirled round.

'Mrs Masters, it's wonderful! Truly, I've never seen or

worn anything like this before. Thank you for letting me try it on.'

'Drink your coffee, dear, or it will be cold. Then sit down here.'

'Oh, but I wouldn't *dare*!' Renata laughed.

'Nonsense. They never crease. You're to go to that party—and you're to wear my dress. I insist!'

Renata drank her nearly cold coffee, and sat down slowly on the settee beside the old woman. 'But I couldn't! I mean, I've already said I won't be going——'

'Pooh! What matter? They'll be delighted. Won't they, Greg?'

It seemed that there was a moment before he replied. 'Why, of course they will,' he answered. Renata glanced up at him. He hadn't moved from the window. She sensed amusement in his face, and felt herself stiffen inwardly. Of *course*! What a fool she was, not to have realised before. Of course he would like her to go. Which was why he had mentioned it to his grandmother, to ensure her intervention. He would like her to go, because he thought, like Virginia, that she would be out of her depth socially, that she would feel gauche and unsure of herself in that brittle throng. He would be watching her, and he would enjoy himself.... She hated him. She kept her eyes on him as he went on: 'There'll be quite a crowd too—one more is neither here nor there for Virginia's mama.' He smiled, he actually smiled. Like the cat that got the cream, thought Renata. Licking his lips at the thought of seeing her fall, metaphorically, on her face. She dared not let her own feelings show. It was quite true, she wouldn't know anyone, but that had never bothered her, anywhere she went, for she possessed the knack—or gift—of being able to talk easily to people anywhere, any time. Greg wouldn't know that. He thought he knew it all, but he didn't know her, not at all.

'It seems I'm persuaded,' she said softly, reluctantly, as though unsure of herself.

'Whoopee!' yelled Christina. 'And you can tell me all about it—in French.' Seeing Mrs Masters' puzzled look, Christina explained about their essays into the French language, and from there the conversation drifted to other topics, and Christina asked about a bicycle, and Greg told her he'd think about it, and wasn't it time she went to bed?

Mrs Masters stood up as well, when he said that. 'I'm tired too, my dears,' she said. 'Christina, you'll walk along with me, will you?' and took her arm. She turned to Renata. 'I do hope you'll read to me again tomorrow.'

'I will. Goodnight, Mrs Masters—Christina. I won't be long myself.' She looked round for her bag as the two went out, for she wasn't staying with Greg. She picked it up, put the empty cups neatly on the tray, and turned to say goodnight to him, but he said:

'Don't go yet, Renata. I'd like a word with you, please.'

CHAPTER SEVEN

RENATA knew, of course, what he wanted to talk about. His favourite subject—the party. Which made it such a surprise when he said: 'I just want to let you know how much my grandmother appreciates you being here.'

She could only stare for a moment. Mentally geared for defence, she was taken aback at being praised. 'Thank you,' she murmured at last.

'And you've already done a lot for Christina. I don't know how you've managed it, but she's smartened up since you arrived.'

'She's a brilliant girl who's never had to use her brain fully. I hope you don't mind me speaking bluntly, Mr M— Greg, I mean, but I just don't feel she's ever been given enough to do. I'm not an expert on children, but I'll help her as much as I can—while I'm here.'

'I'm sure you will.'

She hesitated to mention something that had been on her mind, but as for the moment there seemed to be a kind of truce in the warfare, she took the plunge. 'May I speak frankly?'

His mouth quirked. 'Please do. You have to *ask*?'

She ignored the slight mockery. 'She's fourteen. I think she's lonely. I mean, doesn't she mix with others of her own age? Have any friends?'

Greg sat down, after first indicating that Renata should do so. She sat at one end of the settee, he in the middle, not too near—but near enough. 'That is a problem,' he said. 'She does have a couple of friends, but they're at boarding school. They're two sisters who live nearby. It will soon be holidays, but during term time——' he shrugged. 'I'm afraid, no, she doesn't meet others of her own age.'

'I see. Have you ever considered sending her to boarding school?'

'We've talked about it. Owing to the circumstances of her parents' death, I'm afraid my grandmother is a little over-protective. But——' he shrugged again, 'perhaps you can persuade her.'

'It's not up to me,' Renata answered.

'But I think she'll listen to you,' he said quietly.

'Do you? I've only been here a day.'

'Does that matter? You've already made your personality felt.'

She wasn't sure how he meant it. Mildly spoken, the words could have a double edge to them, and she felt her face tighten slightly, defensively. 'Then I'll do my best, but I won't rush it,' she answered calmly. 'Thank you for telling me what you have.' She began to stand up, and he caught her arm.

'Wait a moment,' he said. It was a gentle touch, not like before. Was it only last night? It seemed years, aeons ago. Renata looked at the hand that rested on her arm, then at him. Greg smiled and took his hand away.

'Is there something else?'

'Yes. Details of the party, that's all.'

'Ah. I wondered when you'd get round to that,' she replied softly. She smiled at him.

His eyes narrowed. 'What do you mean?' he said, equally softly.

'It seems—important to everybody that I go.'

'Only in the sense that we expect you to have time off to enjoy yourself.' She felt the imperceptible heightening of tension, the nearness of him, the vitality he exuded.

'Of course. Very kind of you,' she murmured. 'So what details should I know?'

'I'd like us to leave about nine.'

'Oh. You're taking me?'

'Did you expect to have to walk?'

'No. But what time will it finish?'

'Two—three—four—who knows?' He looked at her, amused, mocking.

'I'll be falling asleep by one.'

'I doubt it. There's usually a lot going on.'

'I'm sure. But as I told you before, I'm not a partygoer. I'm only going to please Mrs Masters—and also, to be quite honest, because this dress is irresistible.' She looked down, smoothed the silky pleats, and smiled. Then she looked up at him. 'Virginia doesn't want me there.'

'Was it so obvious?'

'To me, yes. I can't blame her. I'm a stranger, a member of staff——'

'Does that bother you?'

'It doesn't bother *me*,' she said softly, and could feel the tension building up, because he knew, what couldn't be said.

He drew in breath sharply. 'I see,' he said, very quietly.

Renata stood up. 'I'm not sure you do. But never mind. I'll be ready at nine. Thank you for offering to take me.' She turned away, to walk towards the door, and she wasn't sure if he moved, but she didn't want to talk about it any more, she wanted to leave before she said something she might regret.

But he was behind her. 'Wait,' he said. The room was rapidly darkening now, no lights on, all shadows and soft, disappearing light, and she half turned. They were only a foot or so apart, and she wanted to escape from him because no man had disturbed her before like he could, and she didn't like it. She felt her heart thudding in her breast.

'What is it?' she asked.

'What did you mean—I didn't see?'

'Nothing. Please forget I said it.'

'I don't think you say anything without meaning it——'

'Sometimes. Sometimes I do.' She felt breathless. She wanted to escape, but she couldn't move away.

'No. What did you mean?'

'Let me go——'

'I'm not stopping you.' Of course he wasn't. Renata felt as if he was holding her, but he wasn't touching her at all. She lifted her face to look at him, and he towered over her, even though she wore the high-heeled shoes, and she felt, for the first time in her adult life, small and helpless. It was a new sensation, not entirely unpleasant. She shivered, and Greg put his hands on her arms.

'Are you cold?'

'No.' His touch was warm, electric, sending tingles coursing through her arms, through her body, and now she definitely couldn't move.

'You're shivering,' he said softly.

'It's nothing. This dress is cool.'

'And you're warm——'

'Yes.' The dark air was alive with the tension vibrating around them. 'And so are your hands. Please take your hands away.'

'No,' he said. 'Not until you've told me——'

'There's nothing to tell!' She tried to pull herself away, and his grip tightened imperceptibly, and he pulled her towards him in a slow inexorable movement. Renata put her hands up to stop him, and they encountered a hard chest, and she stopped struggling because it was no use.

Then suddenly it changed. Almost like an explosive quality, the anger was there. 'My God,' he muttered, and released her, almost pushed her from him, and the taut thread snapped, and she was free, and he half turned away. 'You'd better go to bed.' His voice was hard and harsh.

'And you'd better learn to treat your staff more gently!' she snapped, rubbed her arm where his fingers had gripped.

She opened the door and whirled out, obscurely angry herself. She almost ran along the wide corridor, the dress swirling and shimmering around her, to her room, where she closed and bolted the door and leaned against it, getting her breath back. Her anger wasn't for Greg, it was for herself—because, in that moment he had pulled her towards him, she had thought he was going to kiss her—she had wanted him to.

She went over to the window to taste the sweet night air. It was balm to her burning face, and she breathed deeply of it, becoming calmer as the moments passed. It had been nothing, nothing at all. Nothing had happened and nothing would. Except that Greg had been angry, and it was probably because he had nearly lost control. Or was it—she stood very still—was it because he had thought *she* had led him on? She tried to remember the sequence of events, but it was difficult to think clearly. She had gone to the door, to finish the conversation because it was getting too deep, and he had followed, asked her what she meant—then, she frowned, thinking, she had shivered—yes, that was it, and he had held her arms. Then, when she had tried to move away, he had pulled her towards him. Then the world had exploded and he had pushed her away and told her to go.

'Damn you,' she muttered. 'Oh damn, damn, damn!'

She took the dress off, remembering, now it was too late, where her dress and her sandals were, and twisted it up, wincing slightly at what seemed like sacrilege, and laid it on her chest of drawers. Then she went in her bathroom to have a shower.

Minutes after she had dried herself, she was in bed, and moments after that, asleep. It had been a very busy day.

Friday was a no visitors day, when staff were busy cleaning the Towers ready for the weekend rush. Renata had learnt that while the Towers kept a small living-in staff there were

several more villagers who came to clean up before, and
help out with the various shops, and café, on open days.
She had to admire the efficiency with which the place was
run, and after a morning spent reading to Mrs Masters,
went round the entire place with Christina in the afternoon. She was surprised to find a crafts shop which sold
not only local pottery, but silver jewellery at reasonable
prices, another shop selling a profusion of things, including honey, trays, flower perfumes and soaps, tea towels
bearing pictures of the Towers, and paperback books.

Christina had opened the door with the keys her grandmother had given her, and Renata wandered round the
large room delightedly. 'What a lovely shop,' she said. 'I
had no idea this was here.' She picked up a jar of strawberry preserve. 'Can I interest you in some jam, modom?'
she said in fluted tones. Christina laughed.

'Can I interest you in a lovely tea towel with a picture
of Falcon Towers artistically portrayed thereon?' she said,
holding it up with a flourish.

'Well——' answered Renata doubtfully, 'I don't know.
I've got so many already.' She looked round. 'Wouldn't it
be fun to come in on an open day, pretend we're tourists?'

'Would you like to?' Christina's eyes lit up.

'Yes. Why not? Tomorrow? We can go all round with
one of the conducted tours.'

'Gosh, it's a super idea. I never thought of that.'

'Right, we will. Now, let's get some work done, shall
we? French conversation from now on, I think, and what
do you prefer, tennis or swimming?'

'Swimming.'

'Swimming it is. *Allons, mademoiselle!*'

They locked up the shop, went back into the main building to return the keys and get their swimsuits, and went
down to the pool.

Renata had simply forgotten about the party. She had

put it so successfully out of her mind that it was quite a surprise, after dinner, when Christina said:

'If you want to borrow some make-up, you can have mine.'

They were outside, having a walk in the grounds. Mrs Masters had an old friend visiting her for the evening, Greg had been out all day, and the two girls had escaped as soon as politely possible after dinner, leaving the two old ladies talking in the lounge.

'Make-up?' said Renata blankly.

'For the party, you know.'

'Oh! Yes, thanks. That's a lovely idea. But what are you doing with make-up?'

'Uncle Greg bought me a gorgeous box for Christmas. Let's go in and I'll show you. You can have a look at my books as well if you like. Anyway, it's gone eight, you'll have to be getting ready soon.'

'I suppose I will. I'd better wash my hair. Have you a dryer I can borrow?'

'Yes. Come on! It'll be fun getting ready, won't it?'

'Mmm, yes.' No, it wouldn't. But at least, if Christina thought so, the next half hour wouldn't be entirely wasted. Nor the evening, if Renata could observe, and report back to both Christina and her grandmother on everything that happened at the party. And this she intended to do. Only she wasn't aware then of just how the evening would turn out. She had an acute sense of observation, but she wasn't a mind-reader. . . .

Christina's room was a revelation. Posters of pop stars filled two walls, the third was lined with crammed bookshelves, only the wall with the window was plain. Renata looked round appreciatively. 'Very nice, Christina. What a collection of books—can I come and browse some time when we've more time?'

'Of course. Any time you want. Hadn't you better wash

your hair now and it can be drying while you have a look? *Then* you can get the dress on and *then* I'll help you make up.'

Renata hid a smile. 'That's a good idea. I'll get my shampoo.'

'Wash it in my bathroom if you like—I'll find the dryer—oh, have you an evening bag, Renata?'

'No.' She hadn't given that a thought either. ''Fraid not.'

'I'll go and get you one that'll match the shoes. Won't be long.' Christina scrambled to her feet from the cupboard where she had been searching.

'I don't know what I'd do without you looking after me,' said Renata, laughing.

Christina blushed. 'Am I being bossy?'

'No! I meant it! I told you, I never go to parties. I need *you* to tell *me* what I need. I'll go and get my towel.' She went out.

Half an hour later she was nearly ready. It was ten to nine, and she and Christina were putting on the finishing touches with the make-up that had been set out on the girl's dressing table.

'Oh, Renata, that *suits* you,' Christina said admiringly.

'It is rather super make-up,' answered Renata. It was too. A beauty case crammed with Estée Lauder cosmetics of every kind was like treasure trove to her. 'You'll really appreciate this in a couple of years, I can tell you.' She put down the eye-shadow she had just applied. 'Anything else I need, madam?'

Christina giggled. 'Mascara?' she suggested.

'Hmm—why not?' Renata applied the bristly wand carefully, then peered into the mirror. She looked different, she felt different—she felt *good*. Dark lustrous eyes looked back at her. A flawless face, not heavily made up, but subtly so, was there in the mirror, and it was hers. She touched her cheek, smoothing in a tiny blur of blusher.

'Oh, Renata, you look *super*!'

'Thank you.' Renata stood up and did a mock curtsey.

'And you'll tell me everything about the party?'

'Cross my heart.' She took the towel from around her shoulders. Her hair gleamed softly in the sunlight streaming through the windows, the errant curls tamed slightly with hair lacquer. 'Thanks for all your help,' she said, and smiled at Christina. 'We'd better go and find your Uncle Greg, hadn't we?'

'Yes. Come on, let's show Gran first.'

'But of course.'

Greg was waiting in the lounge, holding a glass of sherry and talking to the two old ladies. He was dressed very simply in tight white corduroy jeans and a black silk shirt that was open-necked, and he looked devastating. Very tall, broad-shouldered, long-legged, he turned towards the door as they went in, and looked at Renata. It seemed to her that he caught his breath, but that might have been her imagination.

'Are you ready?' he asked.

'You look simply lovely. Doesn't she look lovely in that dress, Beatrice?' exclaimed Mrs Masters.

'Ah, yes——' Lady Beatrice Lamb, long-time friend of Florence Masters, and of a similar age, looked up from her sherry and gave a reminiscent smile.

'Reminds me of our young days, eh, Florence?' She gazed at the dress Renata wore. 'Remember that party in '28—or was it '29—the one at Cliveden——' She stopped. The two old women looked at each other.

'Ah,' said Florence Masters. 'Ah yes, *that* one——' Smiles were exchanged. Greg took advantage of the pause to say:

'Ladies, I'm afraid we have to tear ourselves away.' He bent to kiss his grandmother's cheek. 'I'm sure your gossip is not for our tender ears anyway. Aunt Beatrice, I'll see you again soon, I trust?'

'Of course you will. Do have a nice time.'

Farewells were said. Christina wandered down with them, to see them off. Greg's Stag was waiting outside the side entrance in the courtyard near the main gates. He opened Renata's door and stood waiting as Christina whispered to her: 'Don't forget.'

'I won't. Thanks for all you've done, Christina.'

The girl stepped back and waved, then they were off. The first few minutes of driving were accomplished in silence, then, as the Towers receded and the wooded drive took over, Greg jabbed the cigar lighter in.

'Mind if I smoke?' he asked.

'Of course not. It's your car.' Renata looked out of the window at the trees flashing past. He seemed to be driving quite fast. She clipped on her seat belt, and saw his mouth quirk, but he said nothing.

'Did you telephone to say that I'd be going?' she asked.

'Yes. I spoke to Virginia's mother. She said she'd be delighted.'

'That's kind of her.' So presumably Virginia knew as well. Renata hid a little smile. She didn't imagine Virginia would be delighted. She hadn't imagined the dislike in those lovely violet eyes. Oh, what the heck, she thought, I've been daft enough to let myself be persuaded to go, I might as well make the most of it. It is an evening out, after all. I'm going to enjoy myself. She sat back and relaxed.

Virginia's home was as large and beautiful as Renata had expected. As they went up the drive—already lined with cars—she remarked on it. The house was of grey stone, the walls covered in trails of ivy, and the drive swept round towards a high columned porchway, with the front doors standing wide open beyond. Greg found an empty space and backed the car neatly into it.

As she opened her door Renata could hear the laughter

and voices from the open windows, and she could see people inside moving around, holding glasses, talking, and there was a fainter drift of music coming from somewhere within the house. Greg locked his door and pocketed the keys. 'Ready?' he asked.

'Yes.'

'Then we'll go in.'

She didn't want to go. Quite suddenly, she didn't want to go to the party at all, and something must have shown on her face, for he frowned.

'Renata? What is it?'

'Nothing.' She managed a smile. He mustn't know. He *must not* know. She walked away from his car, and he followed, and caught up with her. She took a deep breath. Damn him, damn Virginia. This was what they wanted. 'There seem so many people,' she said, aware of how trite it sounded, but unable, for the moment, to think of anything better.

'Scared?' No doubt about the slight edge of mockery in his voice. The word was a subtle taunt, and she felt her face tighten. Wouldn't you love it if I was, she thought. She laughed.

'Heavens! What of? People? I've met enough in the past few years—or didn't I tell you I used to wait on dinner parties?' She looked at him, defiance in her eyes as they approached the wide steps. He seemed about to answer, and then——

'Greg dear, how lovely to see you!' The woman who had appeared as if by magic in the porchway could only be Virginia's mother. Virginia would look just like her in another twenty years or so; still beautiful, but with more weight on her, and perhaps her hair might be silvery grey, as this woman's was.

Greg kissed her, then stood back. 'Chloe, I'd like you to meet Renata Page. Renata, this is Mrs Mannering.'

'How are you, my dear?' The woman's smile was warm and pleasant. She had her daughter's eyes—and the smile hadn't quite reached those, but her handshake was as nice as her smile.

As Renata made the polite responses she was sharply aware of being subtly assessed. She wondered what Virginia had told her mother, and somehow had an idea of what it might be.

'Do come in, both of you. Nearly everyone's here. Greg darling, Ginny's in the library. I'll take Miss Page round and introduce her. Come along, my dear.'

They went in, and as Renata followed Mrs Mannering into the noise filled room to the left of the wide hall, she looked round to see Greg vanishing in another direction. Then they were in the large room, and heads turned, several pairs of eyes looked at her, and one man's stayed on her, then he detached himself from a group and came over.

'Good evening, Renata,' he said. It was Ian, looking very attractive in a cream suit and cream silk open-necked shirt. 'I'll look after Renata, Aunt Chloe,' he added with a grin at his aunt.

'Do introduce her around, won't you?' Mrs Mannering looked vaguely across the crowded room, waved, added: 'Do excuse me, I must——' and vanished.

'You're looking very delectable, Renata.' Ian did a neat turn and lifted two glasses from the tray of a passing waitress. 'Champagne?'

'Thank you.' She smiled at him over the glass. Several men were still watching them, but none of the women—or at least not openly. The talk sounded loud and somehow brittle and she wondered how long she would be able to stand it. There was a loaded table at the far end of the room crammed with bottles and glasses, and two dinner-jacketed men were pouring drinks out as fast as they could as the waitresses returned to fill their trays. The room was extremely large, as big as a ballroom, and there must have been well over a hundred people, clustered in groups, all with drinks in their hands, all talking and laughing. The windows were open, but the room was very warm.

'So you made it then?' Ian looked at her in a way that made his feelings obvious. She wondered if Virginia had told him off for asking her. Probably.

'Yes, I made it.'

'Your dress is gorgeous. I thought you'd nothing to wear?'

'I hadn't. Mrs Masters insisted that I borrow it, and I couldn't resist.'

'Nor can I.' He smiled. 'Come on, I'll take you round. I see you've already made a hit with the gentlemen—especially our Colonel.' He nodded pleasantly towards a silver-haired man who had moved away from a small group and was staring at Renata with a bemused, dazzled look on his face.

The next half hour was a confused blur of names, faces, smiles, handshakes. Of Greg there was no sign. Perhaps, she thought dryly, he and Virginia were browsing through books in the library, smiling to herself at the thought, and a middle-aged dandy straightened his tie and smiled back at her, thinking it had been for him. Her dress was causing a mild sensation, she knew that by the whispers.

She also knew something else. It was not only the conversation that was brittle and shallow, so was the atmosphere. Nothing she could put her finger on, but there. Ian was pleasant, but Renata knew why. He fancied her. He was exerting himself to be utterly charming, but while she found him easy to talk to, she had no stronger feelings than that about him. She had seen Virginia's mother several times, in the distance, had been introduced to her husband, a hard-faced man with a handshake like iron, and met Virginia's younger sister, Charlotte, equally hard, who had frozen her with a glance and barely escaped outright rudeness when Ian had introduced them. Charming girl, she thought, and looked at Ian as he led her out on to a terrace at the back of the house. The trees were festooned with fairy lights, and several spotlights were directed on the walls, and couples were dancing on the lawn in the darkening twilight.

'Tell me,' she said, having to speak loudly over the blaring music from loudspeakers, 'has Virginia any more sisters?'

'No. Why?' He glanced down at her, amused.

'I wondered.' She gave him a sweet smile and he burst out laughing.

'You know, don't you?'

'Know what?'

He swung her into his arms and steered her out on to the grass, away from the loudspeakers and towards the shadowy trees. 'Know that my dear cousin is having a fit of the vapours at me inviting you.'

'Hmm, I'd have to be pretty dense not to have guessed that,' she answered wryly, trying to keep in step with his erratic dancing.

Ian pulled her in among the trees, and here it was pitch black, and they were an unseen audience to the laughing couples dancing on the grass. It was like a moving tableau, brightly lit and noisy, but not so loud that they couldn't talk normally. Ian put his arms round her and kissed her soundly, taking her by surprise. Not that she hadn't expected he would try; she knew he would sooner or later, but she hadn't expected it quite so soon.

She laughed and pulled herself away. 'Really, sir,' she protested. 'Is this what you brought me out here for? Shame on you!'

He kissed her again, effectively silencing her, and when he released her, said thickly: 'God, I've been aching to do that all evening.'

Renata was more intrigued with the unfinished conversation about Virginia. His kisses left her not only totally unmoved, but almost totally indifferent. She wouldn't dream of telling him so. She didn't like hurting people's feelings unnecessarily—except perhaps one person——

'What do you mean about Virginia having a fit of the vapours?' she asked innocently, putting her hand up to Ian's neck in a way that kept him at a slight distance, but let him think that she enjoyed touching him.

He looked at her. 'Hmm?' he murmured, eyes unfocussed clearly not thinking about Virginia at that moment.

She sighed and repeated the question gently. 'Oh. It's obvious, isn't it?' he answered at last as he—almost absentmindedly, it seemed—caressed Renata's shoulders. 'She took one look at you and thought you'd be after her precious Greg—and let's face it, Renata, you've a lot going for you—I do mean a *lot*.' He bent his head to kiss her again, and she sidestepped smartly. 'You are *gorgeous*,' he said huskily, 'absolutely gorgeous—I've never met anyone like you——' He pulled her to him. 'What say we take a little stroll? There's a summerhouse I'd like to show you——'

She put her finger to his lips. 'Ian, dear, I wasn't born yesterday, my sweet, I'm staying here where I'm safe. Heavens!' She fluttered her eyelashes in mock horror. 'How do I know I can trust you? I am but a poor working girl, remember——'

'You're a witch,' he grated, 'who's driving me insane. Come here——' He caught her as she tried to move away, and held her tightly in a pair of strong arms. 'Has *he* made a pass at you yet?'

'Who? Greg?' She laughed. 'You must be joking!'

'It's no joke,' he said thickly. 'He's not made of stone—at least, according to Ginny he's not,' and he laughed.

She didn't want to know any more, she really didn't. 'I think it's time we got back,' she said firmly, and pulled away. 'I want to join in the fun.' And heaven help me for that fib, she thought.

'Fun?' he echoed. 'You'll have more fun out here with me—that I can promise, my sweet—and in any case, I'd keep ever so slightly out of Ginny's way if I were you——' He paused.

'Oh, I will,' she assured him. 'Thanks for the warning. Just don't forget that it was *you* who invited me.'

'I've not been allowed to,' he groaned. 'But, hell, I wanted to see you again—and again. I'm here till next week. How about Sunday? A day out—anywhere you want, just say.'

'Sounds lovely,' she said. Anything to get back inside. 'Phone me tomorrow.'

'Just another kiss before we go,' he pleaded.

'No. You shouldn't ask!'

'Then I'll take——' and he did. Then they walked back into the house. The first person Renata saw, standing on the terrace, glass in hand, was Greg. He was alone, standing apart from the crowd who were dancing, laughing, and by now, singing. He watched them as they walked across the lawn, weaving in and out of the enthusiastic dancers. It was almost as if Renata could read his mind—but if she had been in any doubt the look in his eyes would have said it for him. Then he turned away and walked into the house.

CHAPTER EIGHT

IT was two o'clock in the morning. Renata sat beside Greg in the car as he drove away from the party. He had not said a word since leaving the house. The waves of anger flowed around them in the car like a strong current, and she sat very still, very quiet, evening bag on her knee, and looked ahead at the narrow winding road lit by the beam of his headlights, remembering what had happened. . . .

She too was angry—with him, with Ian, and with herself for being so stupid and blind not to have seen before what was now so obvious. How clever Virginia had been! How very clever. She had had a little plan, and it had worked beautifully—and the fact that Renata was wearing a borrowed, valuable dress must have been a bonus for her that she could not have foreseen. Renata's hands were clenched tightly on her bag as she fought for control. If Greg said one word, just one word, he would regret it. . . .

Then the car was slowing, slower, slower—and he pulled up in a layby and switched off the engine, and she mentally braced herself for the attack, but she was going to play it cool. Very cool. 'Why have you stopped the car?' she asked quietly.

'Why do you think?' His voice was low, taut, tightly controlled. 'You don't suppose it's because I want to gaze at the moon with you, do you? Your tastes are more advanced that that, aren't they? With you it's straight into bed——'

'You've said enough.' She turned to face him. 'I'm trying to keep very calm, Greg, but I'm not going to be insulted by you.'

'You don't have much choice,' he responded, tight-lipped. 'I intend to tell you exactly what I think of you——'

'You've already made *that* very clear,' she flashed back. 'The fact that you chose to put your own interpretation on what you saw is your concern, not mine. If I told you the truth you wouldn't believe me, so I won't even try.'

'The truth? There's not a lot of interpretation I *can* put on it when I walk into a bedroom and see you, with hardly any clothes on, locked in Ian's arms, and both of you obviously drunk——'

'My God!' she gasped, 'how dare——'

'I haven't finished,' he cut in. 'And I dare, all right. I took you there as a guest, and you end up seducing your hostess's nephew——'

Crack! Renata, calm, unflappable Renata, who rarely lost her temper, and had never struck anyone before, had had enough. She lashed out and caught Greg a stinging open-handed slap on his face, then opened the car door during the few seconds it took for him to recover from the shock.

She was several yards down the road when he caught her, whirled her round, and shook her. 'You *bitch*,' he grated. 'You little bitch!'

She swung her evening bag at his face, and followed it with a blow with her elbow on his arm.

'Don't *touch* me,' she breathed. She wrenched herself free and started running back to the car, to the driver's door, which he had left open, and dived in, fumbling for the ignition. She had barely touched the keys before he was in at the other door, had wrenched them out of the lock, and put them in his pocket.

'I warn you,' she said. 'I'll fight—and you'll be sorry——' Then she was silenced as he caught her, pulled her savagely towards him, and kissed her.

She was totally helpless, locked in a pair of arms holding her so tightly that she could barely breathe as Greg punished her brutally with his hard mouth, not once, or twice, but over and over again until she was dizzy with shock. She tried, oh, she tried, to twist her face away from the savage punishment, but in vain. She could hear his breathing, hear too his heartbeats, and feel them against her breast, and her head swam, and it seemed that the car was whirling round—then he released her, pushed her away from him, wiped his hand across his mouth and said huskily: 'And that's just for starters.'

She bent forward, bruised, shattered, and put her face in her hands. Her whole body shook with fear and shock, and suppressed tears. She would not cry. She would not let him have that satisfaction——

Greg put his hand under her chin and turned her to face him. His eyes were dark, his mouth trembled. 'Nothing to say for yourself?' he taunted. 'Be thankful we're in a small car or I'd let you see how I make love. That is what you want, isn't it?'

She couldn't answer. She felt bruised all over as if he had already taken her and raped her. Her mouth felt sore and swollen. But her anger had gone, annihilated in the force of his. She managed to whisper: 'No, you don't understand——'

The shameful tears could no longer be denied. They welled up inside her and overflowed, and she sat there, held by him, shaking helplessly with sobs, her body racked with them—and something changed. In those first few moments, something changed. She heard Greg's wordless exclamation, almost, it seemed to her, of contempt, and he let her go. She sat back in the seat, and whatever he chose to do now, she wouldn't be able to prevent him. She was weak and vulnerable; she had never felt so helpless in her life. With the anger going, there came in its place the desire to explain, to let him see how very wrong he was. His anger had been so violent and shocking that she knew she *must* let him know the truth, at whatever cost to her.

She took a deep shuddering breath. 'I did not go to that bedroom with Ian to make love to him,' she said very quietly. She looked at him as he sat there, his hands braced against the dashboard as if he might strike her if he didn't hold on, and she went on: 'He—Ian, that is, spilled wine down the back of my dress. We were in the hall at the time. He—he'd been showing me the pictures there, the family portraits.' She took a deep breath. At least Greg was listening. 'And when he spilt the wine I was terrified of spoiling the material. No one else was about. Everyone was at the buffet in the dining room. We—we'd just been about to go in ourselves when it happened. He seemed as shocked as me, and I said something like—"I must sponge this off," and he said—"Right, follow me."' She put her hand to her mouth. 'I followed him up the stairs, thinking he was taking me to a bathroom, only he opened a door, and it was a bedroom, with a vanity unit in the corner. "You can get your dress off here," he said, "I'll go and fetch a cloth. No one will come in," and he went out. I didn't stop to think about anything except that the sooner I sponged the wine off the better, before it could mark the material, you understand, so I slipped the dress off and carried it to the bowl, filled the bowl with clean water and began to wipe the material gently with a new handkerchief from my bag. I thought I would have it done before he returned—only he came in as I was still doing it.' She stopped. Her tears had dried now. She was concentrating on getting the exact order of events right, and nothing else mattered except that. She was unaware that her hands were clutching her bag so tightly that her knuckles were white.

'And then he—he came over to me and said something on the lines of—"Is that a bruise on your shoulder?" And he put his arms up to hold me and touched my bra strap, and said—"just there——" and as he did that, you walked in.'

She stopped, drained, and looked at him. 'And that's the truth. I'm quite aware of how it must have looked to you, Greg—but that is what happened. If I'd wanted to go to bed with him, it would have been none of your business anyway, but I didn't. I don't make a habit of making love to strange men—or even ones I know.'

There was a silence following her words, a silence which stretched and grew and became so taut that she could hardly bear it. Then he spoke.

'And you expect me to believe that?' His voice was low and even, very well controlled—but still, unbelievably, angry.

'Yes. *Yes!*' she shouted, her own control snapping. 'Feel the dress—feel it, go on—it's still damp at the back——'

'That's easily done,' he said, 'to cover up.'

'You swine!' she gasped. 'Oh, God, I hate you, I hate you!'

'Move over,' he cut in. 'I'm going to drive us home.' He got out of the passenger seat, slammed the door and walked round the front of the car. Renata slid across, numbed with shock. He did not believe her. He did not——

As he got in, she asked: 'Tell me something. Why did you come in at that precise moment?'

He looked at her, grim-faced. 'Why? I'll tell you *why*. Because someone passing had thought that a woman was being murdered in that room, with all the noise going on, and had asked me to investigate——'

'Noise?' she gasped. 'They must be mad, or drunk. Who was it?'

'It doesn't matter,' he answered, face still grim and hard. 'They'd obviously misheard—or misinterpreted, shall we say, the kind of row——'

'They're lying,' she whispered. Then she stopped. She

knew. Of *course*. There was only one person it could have been—one—a person who disliked Renata intensely after just a few moments' acquaintance, who hadn't wanted her to go.

'Virginia,' she said softly. But Greg didn't hear, because he was starting up the engine, and Renata, her brain functioning now with icy clarity, wondered what part Ian had played in the timing of that little charade. It all fitted now; it all fell into place. Ian had made it very clear that he desired her. He would probably consider it quite a joke to ensure that Greg would certainly not be making any passes at her after what happened.

She wondered if Ian had thought that the scene might well have got her the sack. She sat back, feeling sick with it all. It could still happen. Greg was a very angry man. There was nothing she could say or do to alter his state of mind, nor did she intend to try. Her own innate sense of dignity forbade her to plead for mercy. She despised her own weakness in weeping, but that would never happen again.

She took a deep breath to calm herself, and began breathing steadily and slowly, willing herself to become calmer. The next half hour could be crucial ... Greg drove in silence, eyes straight ahead, profile hard, hands tightly on the wheel. He said not a word.

He drove into the grounds, up the winding drive, into the garage area, and there he stopped the car, leaned over, opened her door, and said: 'Wait here. I'll put the car in.'

Renata waited in the dark cobbled yard, shivering slightly in the cool night air. All was dark and silent, the sky star-speckled, the building heavy with slumber. She heard a car door shut, then Greg's footsteps, and the garage doors closed and he was a dark shadowy figure walking towards her, enormously powerful, a man who had violently assaulted her in his deep anger, and who was still smouldering.

'This way,' he said. She followed him across the yard and through a door which he bolted after them, then they were in a passage lit only by a dim light ahead. Renata walked along it, Greg just behind her, and she could feel his presence like a force, almost as if he were touching her, and she loathed him. She walked with her head held high and eyes dry. Never again would he make her weep. If she had to leave here she would simply find another job as soon as possible. It might take her longer to pay back the debts, but she would do it. But before she went she would see Ian and find out if her suspicions were correct. Strangely enough her loathing for him didn't go as deep. He was probably weak. Despicable yes, but easily led, not strong like the silent shadow at her heels.

She suddenly recognised where they were. They were going up another set of stairs that led to the bedrooms from a different angle of the Towers. She was icily sober. Greg's remark, on top of everything else, that she had been drunk, still rankled. Ian had certainly been the worse for drink; Renata had been as sober then as she was now, having drunk only two glasses of champagne, and one of wine, all evening. She was also starving. She had not made it to the dining room, after what had happened, for at the end of the dreadful scene that had followed, in the bedroom, when Greg had discovered them together, he had said in a voice that brooked no refusal: 'Get your dress on now. I'm taking you home.' He hadn't even glanced at Ian. Ian, who had stood there, not quite smiling—and not saying a word. Renata, sensing the potentially explosive atmosphere, had put on the dampened dress and walked out—because Greg had looked as though he might have killed Ian if he had said a word. He had looked—dangerous. . . .

It was then that she realised how weak Ian was. She had looked at him, seen what was in his face, and turned away. They had walked down the stairs, she and Greg, and there had been no one in the hall, everyone was eating in the dining room, the talk and laughter mingling with the sound of crockery and the fainter music from outside. All that Greg had said was: 'Wait by the car,' and she had gone out, too numbed by what had happened to demur. Minutes later he had come out, opened the car doors, and from then on until the explosive scene, had been silent.

Renata reached her door. Very quietly, knowing that nearby were a sleeping woman and girl, and knowing that he wouldn't risk making a row here, she said: 'I'm very hungry. I didn't get anything to eat. If you'll please just tell me where the kitchen is from here——'

He said something brief and unrepeatable, his eyes cold and hard upon her, then: 'This way.' He turned and walked off, and she followed, across the wide hall, down another corridor and through a door, which he closed after them before switching on the light. They were in a large airy kitchen where everything gleamed, working tops, table top, and huge stove. The fluorescent lighting was brilliant and hard upon the eyes after the darkness, and she blinked. 'Sit down,' he said, and went over to the refrigerator, which hummed softly in the corner. She sat at the table and watched him. She was almost too hungry to care about anything else at that moment, even if Greg was going to tell her to leave tomorrow. ...

'Will chicken do you?'

'Yes.' She took the plate containing thinly sliced chicken pieces from him. 'Thank you. You can leave me here. I'll wash the plate and switch the lights off.' She began to eat. The chicken was delicious—but even dry toast would have tasted good at that moment. Greg turned away.

'Want a glass of milk? I'm having one.'

'Please.' He wasn't going to send her packing. If he had been going to, he would have said so by now. She didn't know how she knew it, but she did. He poured out two glasses of milk and handed her one.

She finished the chicken. 'Had enough?' he enquired.

'Yes, thank you.' She looked at him. She was dry-eyed, calm, and, now that her hunger was appeased, feeling better. 'There's just one little thing I'd like to say. It's this.' Her voice was even and controlled. 'This dress that your grandmother lent me is so beautiful that I could never *ever* damage it or do anything to spoil the material. If you think I could have put water on it simply to make you believe my story of what I was doing in the bedroom, you're making a very big mistake—that I swear to you.' She stood up to carry her plate and glass over to the sink. She had said all she was going to say. In a strange way, that remark of his had hurt her more than all his accusations. If Ian had spilt wine on it deliberately, as she suspected strongly, that was in a way more unforgivable than anything else he had done in the sick charade.

She left the rinsed plate and glass to drain and turned to face Greg as he stood watching her. No longer the shaken, vulnerable woman she had been in the car, she was again in control of her emotions. 'Now, I'm going to bed,' she said. 'I won't thank you for taking me to the party, because it was the worst evening I've ever spent in my life. Good-night.'

She walked towards the door, tall, steady, proud. She felt as if she were walking away from him in another sense. As if, from now on, they would be strangers, one standing at each side of an unbridgable gulf. For he had said, and done, unforgivable things. She opened the door and went out. Greg didn't speak or attempt to stop her, he just watched her go. It was past three in the morning. There was work to be done, later this day, much work, and she was very tired.

She went into her bedroom and took off the dress with great care, then laid it on the bed, preparatory to examining it—and it was then that she saw the note on the pillow. She picked up the sheet of paper and read the message written on it. 'Renata, your brother phoned. He's coming up to see you Saturday or Sunday. Christina. P.S. Hope you had a good time.'

Renata put the note down, and a vague sense of unease filled her. Neil—coming here? She sat down and picked up the dress and began to examine it at the back, but her mind was only partly on the task. If Neil was coming up here instead of phoning again, it would be for only one reason: he was in some kind of trouble. There was only one kind of trouble that Neil ever got into—and that was money. She said, very qietly, in a despairing whisper: 'Oh, God.'

She slept soundly, as she always did, but her dreams were not pleasant ones, and she awoke at eight—an hour late—with the taste of them still within her, and a vague sense of unease making her restless. Greg was not at breakfast, but both Mrs Masters and Christina were agog to hear of the events of the previous night. It was very difficult to speak as though nothing amiss had happened, but Renata managed as best she could, describing the setting, the dancing on the lawn, the people there, even the food, which she had seen, although not personally touched—but she didn't tell them that.

When breakfast at last was over she went down with Christina to join in a tour of the Towers. Still she had not seen Greg. As they went outside through the little gate that led to the swimming pool, so that they could mingle with the tourists already arriving, Renata asked casually: 'What time did my brother phone, Christina?'

'About ten. I took the call.'

'Thanks for leaving the note. Did he say anything else?'

'No-o,' Christina shook her head. 'He seemed a bit anxious to contact you, but he said it was no use trying to get him 'cos he wouldn't be his apartment. But he'll see you today or tomorrow, he said.'

So he wouldn't be at his place. The sense of unease deepened slightly. 'Oh, well, I'll see him soon,' she answered. 'Now, let's see—this is the way we go in, isn't it?'

'Yes. This is going to be good,' giggled Christina. Both girls were dressed in jeans and sweaters and sandals. Christina looked at Renata. 'We look like sisters,' she remarked.

'So we do.' Renata smiled at her and patted her bag. 'We might even buy a tea towel or a pot of jam from the shop.'

The girl laughed. 'You make everything more fun,' she said. 'Honestly, you do. I'd never have thought of this on my own.' They were entering the main hall, and the girl taking money at the desk looked up, startled, when she saw them. Christina put a finger to her lips. A party of four Americans were just ahead of them, studying the guides they had just bought. 'Ssh!' she whispered. 'We're ordinary lookers-round today, Jean.'

Jean grinned. 'Oh, I see,' She handed them each a guide. 'Compliments of the management. I hope you'll find your way around all right, madam.'

'We'll try. Come on, Renata.' A couple with two young boys followed them in, and Christina and Renata set off on the grand tour, behind the Americans.

Renata had been shown round by Christina, but it was different going round on an open day, sauntering with so many others through the high-ceilinged, beautiful rooms, commenting on the stone walls, the furniture, the stained glass windows, and all in slightly hushed tones as if awed by the size of it all. They paused in what had once been a dining hall, and the immensely long oak table was set as though for a meal, and there were bowls of flowers at intervals, and candelabra, and Renata could picture it filled with people of a bygone age, with the candles lighted and a log fire burning in the enormous fireplace. Christina had told her that very occasionally, now, it was used, usually at Christmas when Greg and Mrs Masters would give a party for relatives and friends from all over the world, and the

Towers would once again echo with music and laughter. Renata could picture it clearly. She wondered if she would ever see the dining hall full. Perhaps. . . .

They took their time, they lingered, and they studied the detail in the fine wood carvings that abounded in nearly every public room, then at last they reached the shop, which was crowded with visitors buying gifts for their friends at home. Christina took Renata over to the woman assistant to introduce them.

Mrs Armitage nodded, smiled, apologised. 'Sorry I can't talk,' she said, 'only Margaret's not turned up this morning and I'm on my own——' she darted away to fetch an extra pot of honey for a customer, then returned. 'Lor, it would be on a Saturday as well!' Her voice changed. 'Maps of Yorkshire, madam? In the far corner, bottom of the book rack. So you see——' she was back with them again, 'I'm a bit rushed. Christina love, if you could see your way to fetching me a cup of tea, I'd be ever so grateful——'

Renata looked at Christina, and Christina looked at Renata. 'Shall we?' said Renata, and Christina laughed and said:

'Could we?' and Mrs Armitage looked at them both as if she, or they, had gone mad, only she wasn't sure which, and Christina added: 'We'll help you.'

'You will?' The woman gasped. 'But——' She looked bewildered—but hopeful.

'Yes.' Renata stepped behind the counter. 'Christina, better make that three cups of tea. Now, Mrs Armitage, point me to the till and I'm all yours.'

'Oh, bless you both!' The woman grinned her relief. She was a stocky Yorkshirewoman, dark-haired, rosy-cheeked, and with a ready laugh. As Christina darted off for the tea she pointed out, in between serving, where everything was, and within minutes Renata was serving too.

When Christina returned bearing three cups of tea and

three chocolate wafer bars on a tray, they made Mrs Armitage sit in a quiet corner for a break while they served. Christina was enjoying herself hugely, you could tell, and Renata would have been if it hadn't been for the nagging worry inside her over Neil.

An hour passed, and at nearly twelve they persuaded Mrs Armitage to go and have some lunch. Trade had slackened off slightly. It was such a glorious day that visitors were going outside to sit on the grass insted of browsing too long in the shop, and it was during this lull that Ian walked in. The first thing Renata noticed was the long darkening bruise on his jaw. The second was his black eye and the third was that his eyes searched hers, almost as if fearing to speak to her, before he said:

'Hello, Renata.'

'Hello.' She continued wrapping three tea towels for an elderly woman and her husband. 'Thank you, goodbye.' She smiled at them both, and they smiled back and trotted out happily. 'I'm rather busy, as you see.'

'Yes, I do. Mrs Masters told me you'd gone on a tour of the place and I've looked everywhere else — I didn't expect to see you working here.' He spoke anxiously, pleasantly, as if trying to make a joke; the only trouble was, it didn't quite come off. He was too tense. Renata didn't care. She had no intention of making things easy for him. She gave him a cool pleasant look.

'I rarely do what I'm expected,' she answered softly. Christina was helping a young boy choose a present for his mother, and could not overhear.

'Can I speak to you?'

'You're speaking now,' she pointed out, reasonably enough, she thought.

'In private, I mean.'

She looked at him properly then. No one waited to be served. There were only four customers in, including the boy, and all were browsing happily. 'Why?' she asked. 'To apologise for what you did?'

'Yes.' She was surprised. She had expected to disconcert him, not to hear that very humble yes.

'It wasn't a very nice trick, was it?' she went on. 'I worked it out, you see, all by myself. It was a filthy nasty rotten trick, in fact—and I can guess who put you up to it.' She stared at him, contempt in her eyes.

'Greg came back.' His words stunned her. For a moment she literally could not speak, and wondered then if she had heard wrongly.

'What?' she whispered.

'He came back, after——'

She motioned him to silence as a middle-aged woman came up bearing a handful of postcards, served her, then said: 'We can't talk now.' She looked at her watch. Mrs Armitage had been away nearly twenty minutes. She was due back at any time. 'Wait, will you? When the assistant comes back we'll go outside.'

Ian walked away silently and went over to the bookstall. Renata, watching him, felt her first pang of pity for him. She sensed that it had cost him a lot to come over as he had. She owed it to him at least to speak to him. But what did he mean about Greg going back? That was even more in-triguing than the mark on his chin and the black eye, neither of which he had had last night.

She waited in a fever of impatience, and when Mrs Armitage came in the door, she left the counter. 'I'm going outside for a few minutes,' she said. 'Is that all right?'

'Bless you, love, of course.'

Ian followed her out into the sunlight. There was a long seat under a spreading oak, away from the crowds, and Renata went and sat down. 'I'm only talking to you for a couple of minutes,' she said. 'I'm working in there—and in any case there's not a lot to say on my part because if I told you what was in my mind you'd be very shocked.'

'Renata,' he answered, 'you don't need to. I just came to tell you how very sorry I am. Believe me, I've been plucking up courage all morning to come here. I left Ginny's today, after what happened, and I don't suppose I'll be going back for a long time. But I couldn't go without seeing you—I knew you'd be angry, but I was prepared for that, and nothing you say can make me feel worse than I do already.' He grinned faintly. 'But go ahead, if you want.' He looked steadily at her. 'I deserve it.'

She shook her head. 'I believe you. I accept your apology. What do you mean, Greg went back?'

'The party was nearly over. People were leaving, when he came roaring up the drive in his car. Aunt Chloe thought he'd forgotten something—no one else there knew what had happened, only Ginny and me. He'd told my aunt that you had a headache—he——' he stopped and pulled a face. 'This is painful for me, but I've got to tell you. He came in and asked me, very quietly, if he could have a word with me. I knew——' he looked down at his clasped hands, 'I knew why, by then, because, believe me, I was feeling pretty rotten about the whole thing. I'm not trying to put the blame on Ginny. It was her idea, but I fell in with it, because——' he swallowed. It seemed an effort for him to speak, 'because she's always been able to persuade me into anything—and it seemed a lark, no more, and, oh, God forgive me, I thought it would get you easier into bed.' He stopped at Renata's gasp. 'Only it didn't turn out like that.' He contemplated his hands in silence for a moment. 'I'm not proud of myself. This is agony for me to tell, because you'll hate me and there's nothing I can do about that, but perhaps you'll believe I'm not such a swine as I seemed.' He took a deep breath.

'We went into the library, just the two of us. I don't know where Ginny was, probably seeing some guests off.

She'd been in a foul mood since you and Greg had left, because it hadn't gone to plan. She'd thought he'd send you packing and I'd have to run you home—and of course, on the way home, I'd planned to "comfort" you——' he stopped. 'Well, you know.'

'I know,' she said evenly. 'What happened in the library?'

'Greg just said, "I want the truth about this evening. I want it fast—and I'm in no mood to listen to fairy tales." And he wasn't. He looked—I've never seen him look like that before. He scared me, and I'm not easily scared. I started to tell him, then Ginny came storming in—she must have seen him arrive—and she looked at me as if to warn me, but he just turned round on her and asked her to leave us alone. I've never seen Ginny shrink like she did then. She went white, and she said something about it was her house, and she'd stay if she wanted to, then Greg told her that he knew all about her little game and as far as he was concerned she could go and jump in the lake—and she went mad! She stormed over to me and started hitting me, screaming I was a lousy sneak—and he pulled her away, said to her, something like—"Don't spoil it for me," and as she staggered into a chair he came up to me and said, "I'm going to beat the hell out of you, Mannering," and the next thing I knew I was lying on the carpet, he'd gone, and Aunt Chloe was sponging my face with a flannel.' He took a deep breath and turned to her, stroking his jaw. 'And that's how I came to get these.'

'Perhaps you deserved what you got.' Renata was more shaken than she would admit. Greg had gone back—*gone back*, after giving her the impression that he thought she was a little tramp, and as good as telling her so. For that she would never forgive him. She found it easier to forgive Ian. She couldn't hate him any more, but she hated Greg. Then she looked up to see him crossing the grass towards them. So did Ian, and he stood up, probably on the principle that if he was going to be hit again, he would be in more of a position to defend himself.

'What are you doing here?' asked Greg in even tones. The two men faced each other.

'I came to apologise to Renata. Don't worry, I'm just going. I know this is your land.' Ian turned to her. 'Goodbye.'

She stood up. 'Goodbye, Ian.' She looked at Greg, then back to Ian. 'I'm going back to work in the shop now,' and she turned and walked away from them. She didn't look back. She didn't intend to speak to Greg again, except when unavoidable. She had nothing she wanted to say to him, ever again.

CHAPTER NINE

LUNCH was at one, and there they explained to Mrs Masters what they had been doing all morning. She was at first concerned, then, as Christina's obvious enjoyment of the situation came across, she smiled and nodded.

'Sounds fun, my dear,' she said. 'And how kind of you both to offer! Really, Renata, we'll have you wondering what kind of slavedrivers we are here!'

Renata joined in the laughter. 'I've enjoyed it immensely.' Greg was very quiet. He had spoken, but not to her, yet it hadn't seemed in any way calculated, and certainly Mrs Masters was unaware of anything amiss.

'So can we go back after lunch?' Christina asked. 'The shop closes at four on a Saturday.'

'If you want to, of course. Greg, we'll have to see about a replacement for Margaret if she doesn't come in next week.'

'Will do. I'll have a word with Jarvis later.' He ate his roast beef steadily, as if hungry, which he probably was, thought Renata, if he'd missed breakfast.

'Then can we go swimming?'

'If you like.' Renata smiled at the girl, then at Mrs Masters. 'The book came for me from my friend this morning. Peggy gave it to me before we set out on our tour. I haven't had a chance to look at it yet, but if you'd like to come down with us——'

'I'd like that. Why not? Greg, what about you?'

He looked up. 'I'll be busy today,' he answered. 'But I'll take you there, Grandmother, of course.'

'That's kind of you, dear.' She beamed at them all.

140

'That's settled, then. I'll sit in the garden until the shop closes, and see you at the pool.'

Renata wanted lunch to be over. She didn't want to stay there in the dining room with Greg longer than necessary. Too much had happened; she needed time to digest all that she had heard from Ian, and she had had no chance. Christina wanted the meal to finish, but for a different reason. She simply wanted to get back to the shop. But it was Greg who left first, after all. As he finished the main course, he rose. 'I'll skip the sweet,' he said, 'if you'll excuse me. I must leave now if I'm to be back for four.'

'Tsk! Men!' sighed his grandmother as he went out. 'No consideration—always dashing off. Still, he's usually very busy. Now, tell me more about your morning——'

When lunch was over they helped Mrs Masters down to her chair in the garden, carried the three swimsuits to the swimming pool, and went back to the shop. Renata had given the old lady the book that her friend Diana had sent— it was in fairly large print, well illustrated, and therefore easier for her to read.

Trade was quiet in the afternoon, and at three, when there had only been two customers in the previous half hour, Mrs Armitage told them that they might as well go, and thanked them very much for their help.

The two girls made their way back to the secluded garden where Mrs Masters sat dozing, the book open on the ground. Christina grinned impishly at Renata. 'You wait,' she whispered. 'When she wakes up she'll say she was only resting her eyes. She *never* sleeps through the day, she says.' She tiptoed over to her great-grandmother, leaned over, and kissed her cheek.

'We're here,' she said. 'Have you been asleep, Gran?'

'No, dear, just resting my eyes for a few moments.' She blinked at them both, and Renata kept a straight face, not without difficulty.

They had spent an enjoyable hour in the pool, then made their way back slowly towards the Towers, where the last of the visitors sat sunning themselves or talking. The atmosphere was one of peaceful calm, and Mrs Masters said: 'I do so envy you your little trip round today, my dears,' to which Renata replied:

'There's no reason why you shouldn't do it with us one day, provided that we take it nice and slowly, is there?'

The old lady laughed. 'You'll be having me playing tennis next! Heavens, all this exercise! I thought I was an old woman, taking things easy. Now I find myself going swimming—and, I might add, I enjoyed that immensely—my word, you're doing me a power of good, Renata!'

'That's what I'm here for,' she answered. She wondered where Greg was. They had not seen him since lunch. It suited her very well. The less she saw of him, the better. But she wondered, all the same....

She went to change into a dress before dinner after seeing Mrs Masters safely into the lounge and settled with her tapestry. Christina went back down to see if Mrs Armitage needed any help locking up, although Renata suspected that the fact that Mrs Armitage had an eighteen-year-old son who collected his mother on a Saturday might have had something to do with her decision to offer help.

In her bedroom she kicked off her sandals and stripped off her clothes. Before going into her bathroom she caught a glimpse of herself in her wardrobe mirror, and paused.

She looked with critical eye at the softly rounded curves of her body. Hmm, not bad, she thought, then laughed at herself for the conceit, and went into the bathroom to shower and wash her hair. She shampooed her hair while she was still under the shower—which was a mistake, as she discovered too late, when she got shampoo in her eyes and couldn't see, and slipped getting out, had to grab the towel rail blindly, swearing under her breath all the while.

Reaching for a towel, she went into the bedroom, eyes tightly shut, rubbing vigorously at her face, muttering under her breath at her stupidity—then, hearing the noise, she managed to open her eyes, and saw Greg standing by the door, hand on handle, apparently about to go out, but also, equally apparently, transfixed to the spot.

'Oh! My God!' she exclaimed, and whipped the towel in front of her, at the same moment that he said:

'I'm sorry, I thought you called me to come in——'

'Get *out*!' Her voice shook, her fingers fumbled to secure the towel, which fortunately was bath-sized and adequate, and her eyes stung, streaming with tears caused by the shampoo. Incensed, still half blinded, she advanced towards him, cheeks ablaze with anger and embarrassment. 'How could you have thought that!' she flared. 'I never heard you knock.' He had seen her naked, for however brief a moment. No man had ever seen her with no clothes on before, and that it should be Greg, after he had called her what he had, was not only ironical, it was doubly humiliating. 'Just get out of here!' Her voice shook.

'Your brother's here, that's all I came to tell you.' It stopped her in her tracks. Neil—here! She had forgotten about that note. Since working in the shop, and the scene with Ian, and the swimming afterwards; so much, in such a short space of time, she had forgotten. She sat down slowly on the bed, felt the colour drain from her face, the anger evaporate with the shock of his words.

'I see.' She pulled the towel up to conceal the swell of her bosom from his eyes, scarcely aware of what she was doing. 'I'll be ready in a few minutes. Where is he?'

'Talking to my grandmother.' Alarm flared, and she looked up. Dear Lord, suppose he had forgotten about the name? Strachan was not a common one, and even if Mrs Masters didn't connect it with anyone particular, she

might find it odd that Renata's surname was different—
and she might mention it to Greg . . . .

'What is it?' he inquired softly, but his face was hard,
very hard.

'Nothing. Please go. I can't change with you here.' She
sat very still, willing him to leave.

'There's no rush. She's entertaining him—he's being
entertained. I want to speak to you privately.'

'I don't.' She looked up at him. 'Certainly not as I am,
but I don't want to speak to you anyway. You said it all as
far as I'm concerned at two o'clock this morning.'

'Then go and put some clothes on, because I'm not leaving until——'

'Ian did all the talking I need to hear. I know that you
went back—and I can put two and two together. You went
because you realised I spoke the truth when I told you I
couldn't, under any circumstances, deliberately damage a
dress like that one of your grandmother's. But you hadn't
believed me before when I protested my innocence, had
you?' Her eyes met his, and she didn't hide the contempt in
them. 'Do you think I'm stupid? I may only be an employee
here, *Mr* Masters, but not you nor anybody can say things
like that to me and get away with them. You are despicable,
and so is——'

She got no further. White-faced, shaking, he stepped
forward and pulled her to her feet, and silenced her with
his mouth. She struggled, aflame with anger—and a
treacherous excitement. She tried to push at him, and the
towel became loosened as she tried desperately to hold it
with one hand while striking at him with the other. She was
sick and angry with herself and with him, because now,
suddenly, she knew something that she should have known
before, and it was the reason that her treacherous body was
disobeying her mind, and she knew why she had stopped
struggling even as she became aware that she had done so.

Her arms went up, not to strike him, not that, but to hold him to her, and she hated herself for doing so, because she hated him—it was possible to despise a man at the same time as wanting him, and she wanted him——

'Dear God,' he whispered, his voice muffled as he nuzzled her hair, and his hands were vibrant and alive on her soft body. 'Dear God, but you're driving me insane——'

His lips came down on hers, and now, not like before, now, like nothing she had ever known in her life, searching, infinitely tender, filling her with warmth and trembling weakness as she felt the pounding of his heart, a hammering against her near-naked body. The sensation of timelessness, of being in a floating space, filled her, and it was as though nothing else existed, or could ever exist, ever again. Her pulses pounded to match his as his mouth, his eager lips explored her face, her neck, her breasts, and she moaned softly, lost in the wonder of being in the same world as him.

She made a throaty, wordless murmur of ecstasy, of love, but no words were needed, none spoken, for there were only the two of them, here, now, in the whole world, and perhaps there was no world, just two beings, as one, all touch, all sensation—lost....

'Renata? Are you there? Can I come in?'

Ice-cold reality struck like a lightning bolt. Shock waves, then——

'No! I'm—not—changed——' She could scarcely speak. She wasn't sure how she got the words out, but they must have been coherent, for as Greg held her, stopped her from falling to the floor, she heard Christina's reply.

'Okay, I'll wait. Only your brother's here.'

Renata managed to point to the bathroom, and closed the door after him. She could not look at him. She found her dress on a chair and fumbled it on, then went to open the bedroom door. Christina stood there beaming all over her face. 'He's nice,' she said. 'He's talking to Gran. She said she sent Uncle Greg to tell you——'

'He shouted me, only I was just going to have a shower. M-my hair's not dry. I won't be a moment now. Will you go back and tell him?'

'Okay. Is he married?'

'No. And he's too old for you! He's twenty-eight. Off you go, you little minx!' Renata closed the door, and waited until Christina had gone, then went to the bathroom door and opened it. She didn't look at Greg. She didn't want to look at him ever again. She had betrayed herself.

'She's gone. Please go.' She kept her eyes fixed firmly on the carpet. She heard his indrawn breath, felt his hand touch her on the chin, and jerked herself free. 'Go,' she breathed. '*Go!*'

He went, and she closed the bedroom door after him, then sank on to the bed, her legs giving way. For a few moments she sat there, numb and trembling and totally unable to move. If Christina had not arrived at that moment, she knew full well what would have happened. It would have been as inevitable as night following day. She put her hand to her mouth. Her fingers shook with a fine tremor. 'Dear heaven,' she whispered. She had so nearly made all his accusations come true.

Shaken and trembling, she finished dressing, and walked slowly out towards the lounge and towards whatever problems awaited her there.

Her worst fears were confirmed after dinner. Neil had been invited, and had accepted, Mrs Masters' invitation to stay the night. He had charmed both her and Christina before and during dinner. With Greg the effect was clearly slightly different, but he had been the perfect host, and Neil had responded, and the conversation had been light and interesting, no strain, and Renata had even managed to eat some food. She had not once, during the meal, looked directly at Greg. She would have found it physically impossible, even had she wanted to, for a deep sense of revulsion filled her— a feeling totally alien to her, for never before had she behaved so wantonly or even been tempted to. That, and her concern about Neil's reason for coming, mingled and made her feel thoroughly wretched. It was only by supreme concentration that she managed to hide her innermost feelings.

Now, dinner over, she walked down with Neil to show him the grounds. Once safely alone outside, he said: 'Renata, I'm in a bit of a fix.' His eyes pleaded with her for understanding, and she turned to him.

'You usually are, Neil. What is it this time?' They were nearing the bench where she and Ian had sat only hours before, and she went to sit down. She had had enough knocks for one day.

'Money.' He sat beside her. 'Oh, God, I've been a fool!'

'That's what you always say.' She looked at him in despair. She loved him because he was her brother, but it didn't stop her wanting to wring his neck at times. 'Neil, when are you going to grow up? And how the hell do you think I can help? I don't imagine you've come all this way solely out of brotherly love, so don't try and tell me you have. Just tell me the worst. How much, and who to? I don't want to know how, because I've already guessed——'

'It's only a couple of hundred,' he said. 'Only I haven't got it.'

'A couple? You mean two hundred?'

'Well—er—not exactly——'

'How much, *exactly*?'

'Five hundred.'

'Oh, no!' She clasped her hands tightly. 'And I suppose you've come to ask me for it?' She jumped to her feet and stared at him. 'Neil, you're totally irresponsible! You make

me sick! I'm trying desperately to save money to pay all
Father's debts off, and then you come along with this——'

'I know. It'll never happen again,' he began, and she cut
in:

'That's what you say every time.' She whirled away.
'You'll have to give me time to think.' Five hundred
pounds. Not a fortune, admittedly, but enough to set her
back. It had happened before, and it undoubtedly would
again, despite his good intentions. She needed to be alone,
to try to work something out. 'Walk round on your own. I
need to think——' she stopped. What was the use? 'Just
leave me, Neil, please.' She turned and walked away from
him. She didn't realise that she was going in the direction
of the swimming pool until the building loomed up. It was
private in there. In the house itself, even if she went to her
room, Christina might come along to call her. Here no one
would know and she would have time to be alone, to think.

She went inside, and the air was warm and humid. The
water was very still, gleaming faintly green in the sunlight
slanting in through the glass roof. Renata sat on a bench
at the side and looked at the pool. Neil had been gambling.
Whether on horses, or cards, or at roulette, seemed immaterial; the end result was the same. He needed five hundred pounds which he hadn't got and she had, and he had
come to her for rescue. She could refuse. . . .

She took a deep breath. If she did, it might be a valuable
lesson to him. He would have to work to pay off the debt
himself, whereas, if she paid it for him, it would happen
again, and again. . . .

It was quiet here, she was alone with her thoughts, and
she gradually became clearer in her mind about it, and decided what she would tell him as soon as she could. He
wouldn't like it, but it was time he grew up and learned the
value of money, and if this was the only way to do it, so be
it. She closed her eyes, knowing his shocked reaction in

advance, not liking what she had to do—then she heard
Greg's voice saying her name, and opened her eyes to see
him walking towards her from the door. The other, disturbing memories rushed back and she caught her breath, all
thoughts of Neil forgotten, and stood up quickly.

'I'm just going——' she began, and he cut in, effectively
stopping her in her tracks:

'I know why Neil's here.'

'What?' She felt the blood drain from her face. 'I—
don't——'

'It's quite simple. Sit down, Renata.'

'No.' Breathless, she took a step back as he moved nearer.
'No——'

'Don't be stupid!' His voice was suddenly harsh. 'I want
to talk.'

'I don't,' she responded, stung by his tone and the quick
anger in it. Almost as if she had been to blame for what
nearly——

'You're safe,' he grated. 'Sit down.' And there was that
in his face, and in his eyes, which was so overpowering that
she felt herself stupidly obeying. It was a bleak hardness
that brooked no refusal, and she was unaccountably frightened by what she saw.

He sat beside her, not near, not far. 'Neil is in trouble,'
he said.

'He usually is.' She couldn't help the bitterness. 'But it's
nothing to do with you.'

'Isn't it?' He said the words very levelly, very calmly,
and she caught her breath at the sound of them, as if—as
if they meant far more than was on the surface, and she said
very quietly:

'What do you mean?' Her heart was hammering.

'He hasn't told you?'

'I don't know, do I? Until you tell me what he's told
you,' she answered.

'He "borrowed" the money from work——' he stopped at her gasp. 'I see. He didn't tell you that.'

It was a nightmare. No straightforward gambling debt, but theft. *Theft.* She seemed to hear his next words as though from far away. She heard them, but they weren't registering, as he explained how he had persuaded Neil to tell him, because he had guessed something was wrong. Then Greg said the next, fateful words, and they registered. Each one drummed into her bemused senses with bell-like clarity. 'Because, of course, I know why you're here, and why you feel so strongly about paying back your father's debts——'

It was too much. Ashen-faced, Renata rose to her feet, to escape, to get away from the numbing dismay of what she was hearing, but he stood too, and said: 'You can't run away——'

'No! Leave me,' she gasped, and turned, but Greg took hold off her arm and held her tightly.

'You little fool!' he exclaimed. 'You'll fall in——' But she was beyond all reason or sense, and struggled blindly to escape, knowing only that his nearness disturbed her far more than anything else that had happened. She struck out, twisted, wrenched herself free, and started to run— only she had lost all sense of direction, dazzled by the evening sun slanting in, and her foot slipped and she felt the ground vanish from beneath her feet and was spinning, swirling, falling, and then down into the cool green depths of the water.

CHAPTER TEN

RENATA was momentarily stunned by the impact of the water and felt it rush over her head, then the world was green and frightening and she couldn't breathe—until instinct and training reasserted themselves and she kicked out and up, and surfaced. Greg held out his hand and pulled her up and safely out, and she began to shiver helplessly.

'You little fool,' he said, only his voice wasn't angry, it was almost gentle, for him. He picked her up and carried her over to the changing rooms where he sat her down inside the largest and said: 'Strip off your clothes.' Then he vanished. Renata thought that he had left her for good, and peeled off her soaking dress, with difficulty, for it clung to every inch, and she was shivering and cold. Then he was in with her again, holding a large towel, and he crouched down, put it around her bare shoulders and pulled her to her feet.

'Don't talk,' he said, 'and don't argue, because I've just about had enough from you, do you understand?'

She looked up at him, her face and hair drenched, opened her mouth to speak, then closed it again. She wore only her bra and pants. Respectable—and yet not quite, for they were of thin nylon, and while the towel was around her it was all right, but she had no strength, none at all, and while Greg didn't look angry, he might be at any second, and she didn't want him to be. She wanted to go and lie down somewhere in a warm bed, pull the covers up, and let the world go by and leave her alone.

'That's better,' he said. 'You're learning,' and he began

to rub her with the towel, her face, her arms and shoulders, her hair, and he wasn't being rough and he wasn't being particularly gentle, but at least she was getting dry, even if he was far too near, and this was a confined space, and the door was closed, and no one near, just the two of them, and the memory of what had so nearly happened suddenly an overwhelming one within her. He said quietly: 'Turn round,' and she did so, and he began to rub her back, and round her waist, and she stood there letting him do it.

He was inches away, that was all, and the warmth of his hands came through the towel; they burned her with a fire that she dared not admit, even to herself, and she gave a wordless exclamation as she felt her bra fastening snap, and he said something, she wasn't sure what, only to the effect that it had caught in the towel, and she put her hands up instinctively to shield herself. He said: 'It would be easier to get you dry if you took it off, wouldn't it?' and as he said it he eased her bra off, and she had no defence now, none at all, and no escape, for where could she run to like this? She half turned and said, in a whisper:

'Let me dry myself, please.' He took his hands away instantly, as if he too was suddenly aware of the warmth and fire, and murmured:

'Oh, dear God——' then it was too late because she was in his arms. She didn't know how it could have happened, except that for one second she had fallen off balance, and Greg had caught her——

She tasted the sweetness of his lips again, and his hands upon her, and she revelled in the sensuous touch, her body suddenly afire with the pent-up longing from before, all the world lost. . . .

Yet even though she was lost, and she knew that his desire was greater than hers, that he wanted to make love to her more than anything else in the world, for his mouth, his hands, and his body told her so, this was not the place, could not be the place—and, drugged, her senses reeling, and barely capable of moving away from him, yet knowing she must, she murmured: 'No, not—here——'

His mouth stilled upon the pulse in her throat, and she heard his breathing become more shallow, then: 'I know.' It was a broken whisper, a sigh, no more than that.

'You must go.' She could scarcely utter the words, and Greg made a low, throaty murmur in response, a protest, and moved frantically back to look into her eyes, a man as beyond reason as she—more so. It was there in his eyes for her to see, and she wondered if he could also see into her mind and know that she loved him, so she closed her eyes, lest he should, and he kissed her closed lids.

'No,' he said—and bent his head, his tongue a trail of sweet fire down her skin until he reached her mouth, where he stopped to kiss her lips. Then a voice, Virginia's voice, echoed round the pool:

'Greg? Are you in there?'

Renata felt the shock waves vibrate around them with the harsh intrusion, and she stiffened, pulled herself free, looked at Greg wide-eyed, saw the shock mirrored in his own face, and felt her heart pound in irrational fear.

'Greg?' Clicking footsteps on the tiles. No time to think.

'Stay there,' he said. Renata saw him take a deep breath, then he opened the cabin door and went out, closing it firmly after him.

'Virginia? What do you want?' His voice moved away, and Renata began to dress as silently as possible, after first rolling up her sodden dress in the towel, praying desperately that Virginia wouldn't come bursting in.

She squeezed the rolled up dress hard inside the towel, heard Virginia's next words as if in a dream, as if it were not really happening:

'Are you alone?' Her voice had an edge to it. Not shrill, not quite, but not controlled either.

'Why?'

'Because I must talk to you—darling.'

Their voices were fainter now. Renata could almost place them, near the door. Greg's next words were calm, almost level, almost as if nothing had happened. 'I said it all this morning. There's nothing more——'

'But I want to explain—please, darling, let me explain——'

Renata didn't want to listen, but she had no choice. Sound carried clearly over the water. She wondered fleetingly what, if anything, Virginia had heard as she came in, and a pulse hammered in her throat. Very silently she pulled on her dress, as quickly as she could.

'No. We're through, Virginia.' Greg's words were like hammer blows, sharp, decisive, hard—then she heard the woman's anguished cry, heard what happened next, and knew, even though she couldn't see, that Virginia was trying to hold him.

'No, don't say—you don't mean it—Greg darling, it was a joke—just a silly joke——'

'That isn't how I saw it.'

'But—please listen. Ian thought it up——' Their voices moved away, and Renata heard the door open, then close. Silence. She counted ten, then opened the cabin door.

She could see them walking away, very faintly through the glass panels, Virginia clinging to Greg's arm as if she was trying to hold him back. Then they stopped. Renata rubbed her hair, put on her still soaking sandals, and when she looked again they had disappeared. She wondered if Greg had made love to Virginia—and if so, where. Certainly not here—but somewhere warm and safe, where they would be undisturbed, perhaps away on a weekend.

Reason was returning. Sense prevailed, her heart was slowing its frantic beat. She could still feel the excitement, the pulsing memory of his touch, but she was quickly returning to something approaching normal, and with the return came other memories—memories of his words that had so panicked her as to make her lose balance and fall in the pool. What had he said? He had told her that he knew why she was here—but then there was more. As she remembered his final words her heart started to beat faster again, for he had said that he knew why she felt so strongly about paying off her father's debts.

She sat down on the small seat. The words echoed and re-echoed in her head. Greg knew. He *knew*. He must know, then, who she really was.

She managed to make it to her room without being seen by anyone. Safely there she changed into a dressing gown and dried her hair. All her movements were mechanical, her mind dazed with the impact of what she had heard. She walked round the room, needing the physical exercise to prevent her from thinking—but nothing could blank out the shock impact of what had happened. Incident upon incident, like layer on layer—Greg's previous lovemaking, here in her room, Christina's interruption, Neil's shattering news, followed by Greg's words at the pool, the aftermath in the cabin—then finally Virginia's arrival, and her pleading——

It was too much for anyone to be reasonably expected to take. Renata felt ill, something so rare as to be almost unheard of; her head ached with a dull throbbing sensation, and she put the dryer and brush down, put her head in her hands, and wept.

The tears provided a release to a certain extent, so that when the familiar voice of Christina came outside her door, followed by a brisk tap, she was able to say, 'Come in,' in a voice that was nearly normal.

'Oh, Grandma wondered where you were.' Christina stood just inside the door, and looked at her, clearly puzzled.

Renata managed a smile. She wasn't sure how, and it was

probably a feeble effort, but she made it. 'I'm sorry,' she answered, 'but I've got a fearful headache, and I hate to bother anyone, so I just came in here. I should have told someone, I suppose.'

The girl's eyes widened. 'Gosh, I'm sorry,' she said, and went to sit beside Renata on the bed. 'Can I get you anything?'

Renata nodded. 'I'd love a cup of tea and a couple of aspirins, if you wouldn't mind.'

' 'Course I don't!' Christina's eyes were filled with warm sympathy. 'You just stay there. I'll go and explain to Gran. And don't worry—I'll look after you.'

'Thanks, you're a good pal. Where is everyone?'

'Well, Gran and Neil are chatting away. Uncle Greg went out—I thought he'd gone to find you, only then *she* arrived,' Christina pulled a little face, leaving no doubt whom she meant, 'and went to find him, and they've not come back yet.'

'Oh, I see. Will anyone mind if I stay here now? I think an early night would do me good, just as long as you explain to Neil that I've got this rotten headache, and I'll see him in the morning——'

'Oh, that's all right. He's staying till Monday anyway. Isn't that super? And he's taking me riding tomorrow—I like him, he's smashing!' Christina stood up, not aware of the effect of her words. Monday? Renata had to know one thing.

'That's lovely,' she managed to say. 'It's very kind of your grandmother to ask——'

'Oh, it wasn't Gran who asked him, it was Uncle Greg.' She went towards the door. 'I'll only be a minute, Renata. You just get into bed and relax. I'll look after you.'

Then she was gone. Renata stared at the closed door, stunned. Greg had invited Neil to stay. Greg? She didn't like it. She didn't know what it was, but she didn't like it.

She felt a sudden, dreadful uneasiness wash over her. She laid her hand to her forehead to try to stop the pounding in her temples. It was a great effort to put on her night-dress, crawl into bed, and wait for Christina's return.

The cool evening air moved the curtains in a slight breeze, and it grew darker very gradually. Renata awoke from a light doze, and for a moment wondered where she was. The headache had nearly gone. Christina had brought in tea and aspirins, Neil had looked in briefly while she was still there, and there had been something different about him as he had asked how she was, something so changed that she suspected he had called in deliberately while Christina was there so that Renata would not be able to question him or say anything of a private nature. She had the vague feeling that she was being excluded from something, but from what, she had no idea.

There was a tap on the door, Christina's tap, and Renata called out for her to come in. 'I've brought you something to eat, and a glass of warm milk,' Christina told her, carrying a tray in with great care.

'You'd make a good nurse.' Renata sat up in bed, and Christina laid the tray on her knees. 'My word! What's this?' She peeped into a sandwich on the plate.

'Chicken. I made them myself. And some chocolate biscuits.' The girl beamed. 'I thought you might be peckish. Neil and Gran are having supper and watching a film on television, and Uncle Greg's out.'

'Oh.' With Virginia? Perhaps, after all, they had made it up. But she didn't want to think about that. 'Sit down, and thank you. Want one? There's too much here for me —lovely though these sandwiches look.'

'Well——' Christina absentmindedly took one of the biscuits and began to nibble it, 'I am a bit hungry, I suppose. P'raps I will force a sandwich down as well.' She stared at Renata with concern on her face. 'Are you better?'

'Yes, much. The headache's nearly gone. I'll be fine tomorrow.'

'You're having the day off, Gran says. You're to lounge about and do *nothing*, she says——'

Renata burst out laughing. 'I wouldn't know how! But thank her anyway. Tell you what, why don't I measure you for that outfit? Then I can cut it out while you go riding with Neil?'

'Would you? Gosh, you're super!' Christina bounced off the bed and went to the window. 'That tunic thing—and slacks to match?'

'If you want, yes. If we get up early I can make a pattern for the tunic—you'd better find me lots of paper, preferably tracing paper. Do you have any?'

'Think so. I'll go and look when I take your tray. Thanks, Renata, you're a brick.' She twirled round and struck a model-girl pose. 'Ta-ra!' she exclaimed in ringing tones. 'Miss Christina Masters, modelling our latest ensemble from the House of Page——'

There came a sharp rapping on the door, and her words died out. Renata knew who it was. She didn't even need to hear Christina's, 'Uncle Greg!' as she opened the door, to know.

'May I come in?'

Christina held the door wide open, and in he walked. Instantly the atmosphere changed. He looked across at her. 'You're not well?' he asked.

'I had a headache, that's all. Christina is very kindly looking after me.'

'I see.' He ruffled the girl's hair as she stood patiently—and clearly rather puzzled. 'And a good job you're doing too. But your grandmother seems to think it's time you went to bed. Off you go. I'll take the tray. I want to speak to Renata.'

Renata did not want to speak to him. She most definitely did not, but it would be difficult to tell him so with Christina there. The girl pulled a face. 'Oh, all right,' she said, and turned to Renata. 'Sleep well. I'll be up early, I promise.'

'Right. Thanks for everything. Goodnight, Christina.' She watched her leave, and Greg shut the door after her, then came back to the bed, and asked, in very level tones: 'And have you really been ill enough to spend the evening in bed?' The air became charged with the undercurrents she recognised so well. Not the kind there had been at the pool, but a kind of smouldering anger—and something else that she didn't fully understand.

She tried to look calmly at him. She tried, but she didn't succeed. 'Yes,' she answered. 'I don't tell lies.' There was a warmth in her cheeks.

'Except about names, perhaps?' he asked. She felt the blood rush to her head, making her almost dizzy, and she caught her breath.

'What—do you mean?'

He picked up the tray, put it down on the carpet, and sat on the bed. 'Oh, surely you know,' he said. 'Or should I remind you? Doesn't the name Strachan mean anything any more?'

'Neil told you,' she said tonelessly.

'No, as a matter of fact he didn't. He didn't need to. I recognised him—but I made sure of it with a couple of phone calls tonight.'

'All right.' She stared at him. There was nothing to lose now; the game was already lost. 'So you know who I am—and you know why I'm here, so you can stop playing your little games. You've had your bit of fun at my expense. I'd like you to get out of my bedroom, Mr Masters. Even if you make me leave in the morning, this is still my room for the moment.'

'What makes you think I'm going to send you away?'

'Aren't you?'

'No.'

'Then——' she was confused. 'But——'

'I have no intention of letting you go. Dear me, did you think that?' There seemed to be, to her sensitive ears, a note of mockery in his voice. 'You're far too valuable, Renata. You've only been here a few days and already you've done wonders. No, I wouldn't send you away. I even think, odd though it may seem to you, that your motives in coming here, working for *us* while saving to pay your father's debts, are noble, and to be admired.' He looked at her, dark eyes steadily upon her, and they weren't angry. 'I asked Neil to stay on over the weekend. I made him tell me about the money—and on Monday I'm going to London with him to sort everything out.'

His words fell upon her stunned mind, and they didn't seem to be making sense. 'I—don't understand,' she whispered.

'Then I'll explain. The reason I recognised him is quite simple, Renata. It's because—and here we get into the realm of incredible coincidences—the firm that he works for, and has "borrowed" the money from, is one in which I happen to be a major shareholder. Or did you already know that?'

She didn't, but she should have, because Langonn Electronics had been one of the companies her father had been involved with, years ago—and she had sensed a connection with the Masters family then. She had quite simply forgotten about it. She felt as if her world was turning topsy-turvy. She felt almost faint, but it was essential that she keep a clear head, for she sensed that there was something else to come. What it would be, she had no idea, but she had had enough shocks, one more wouldn't make much difference. Only there she was wrong.

'I'd forgotten,' she admitted. 'I don't understand why you of all people are going to London with him—why?' She raised anguished eyes to him, and what she saw in his made her heartbeats quicken, her face go warm.

'It's because,' he said very slowly, as if choosing each word with care, 'I want you.'

She thought she would die. She hadn't heard right. She couldn't have. He was saying—what was he saying? He wanted her. *Wanted* her.

'You mean—you mean—if I let you make love to me— you'll settle Neil's debts?' She could hardly say the words. Her voice shook with contempt.

'What do you think?' The corners of his mouth twitched as if with silent laughter. At that moment she hated him with all her heart. It gave her the strength and impetus to reply.

'I'm not for sale.' She said it quietly and with great dignity.

'Everyone has their price,' he remarked.

'Not me.' She grabbed her dressing gown and put it on, then got out of bed and walked steadily to the door. 'Get out!'

But he stopped her before she could open it by the simple expedient of putting his hand on it. Renata took a deep breath.

'Let me open this door.'

'No. I haven't finished.'

'You have. You just finished it a moment ago. I have nothing more to say to you.' She turned her body slightly to look up at him. 'I meant what I said. Everyone else may have their price, but not me. I wouldn't let you touch me again if you gave me a million pounds—not that you're likely to—but I wouldn't, I swear it. And I will sort out my brother's problems—*me*—because if that's part of the price I don't want to know——'

'Have *you* finished?'

'Yes. Please go,' she said.

'I said I want you. I didn't ask to "buy" you. I want you to be my wife.'

There was a silence after his words. It grew and grew, and she couldn't have broken it for all the world. Then he added, gently: 'What have you got to say to *that*?'

'You're—you're mad,' she whispered at last.

'On the contrary, I'm very sane. I will pay off all your father's debts, and I will put the fear of God into Neil, and do as much as possible to ensure that he's unable to ever get himself in a mess again—and you'll stay here and carry on what you're doing.'

'That is—it's almost the same as buying——' she began.

'No. It's—let's say, a business arrangement—but you will be my wife, and share my name and my home.'

'And sleep with you?'

'Yes.'

'Because you *want* me?' she asked, and didn't attempt to hide the scorn. 'No, thanks! I have no intention of getting married, ever. And especially not to a cold-blooded man——'

'In name only?'

'What?'

'I said—in name only. If not any other way, then that.'

She lifted her chin. 'Why? If you want me? Why?'

'I have—reasons.'

'Then tell me what they are.'

'You have a right to know.'

'How *kind*,' she murmured, honey-sweet, voice edged with acid. She was still too shaken to say more.

'You'd better sit down,' said Greg.

'I'll stand.'

'I think it might be better if you sit.' And then he added: 'Please, Renata.'

His tone was different. The mockery that had so infuriated her was not there any more. He was suddenly very serious. She went over to the bed and sat on it. Greg didn't sit beside her, he pulled up a chair instead, and sat opposite her. He began to speak very quietly—and, after the first few moments of shock impact, she listened without saying a word.

'My grandmother is dying of cancer. She has a year to live, no more, perhaps not even that. She doesn't know it, and I don't intend that she should. It was started by her fall, most probably—whatever reason, it's there. Her dearest wish is to see me married—I know that, but until recently I wasn't prepared to commit myself for life to any woman. I love my grandmother dearly. She's a kind, intelligent woman who guided me when I was younger, who was always there—that, however, is not of direct concern to you. What is, is this. I've seen how, in only a few days, she's become very fond of you. More—you've brought Christina out of her shell in a way that's given my grandmother a great deal of comfort. She's old, she's sick—far sicker than she realises, and yet you've given her a kind of hope for the future. She worries about us—she always has —yet in you she sees someone who will take that burden of worry from her—and that, Renata, is why I'm asking you to marry me.'

Renata sat very still, looking down at her hands, unable to look up at him because her eyes were filled with tears, and all she saw was a blur. She had vowed never to let him make her weep again, and she wept not for him but for the woman she had come to regard almost as a grandmother herself in the past few days.

Greg put his hand forward and lifted her chin, saw the welling of tears that now spilled out, and drew in his breath softly. 'Ah, forgive me. I had to tell you.'

'I'm so sorry,' she whispered.

'So am I. And now you know why I'm asking. Not for myself, but for her. Perhaps that's selfish of me too, to want to see her happy, I don't know. If it is, forgive me for that too. I respect your principles. No, I will not buy you—I will not insult you again by even suggesting it. But until she dies, will you consent to become my wife—in name only?'

He stood up and carried the chair back to its place. 'I don't expect your answer now. But I will tell you one thing, Renata. Whatever you say, whether yes or no, the fact of me helping your brother will not alter. I've given him my word.'

He turned and went towards the door. Tall, powerful, with a dignity beyond his years, he didn't look back at her until he had opened the door and said: 'Goodnight.'

She stood up. 'Wait!'

He paused, hand on handle. 'Yes?'

She swallowed. 'Close the door, please.' Greg closed it softly. He looked at her from across the room, and neither of them moved.

'Yes, I will,' she said.

'Thank you. You'll have no cause to regret it, I promise you.' He seemed to hesitate, then walked slowly towards her. 'I—this is difficult for me to say—but at the pool today——'

'There's no need——'

'Yes, there is. I was—I behaved very badly, but you need have no worry. It won't happen again.' He looked down at her, and she wanted to cry out, to tell him, because couldn't he *see*, didn't he *know*? But all she could do was stand there. For the first time in her life she knew no words to express what was in her heart, because it had never happened before. Wordless, the tears running down her face, she could only look silently at him. He reached out and touched her cheek gently, stroking away a tear. 'It will be all right,' he said. 'You'll see.'

Then he was gone, and she was alone. She touched her cheek where his fingers had rested for a brief moment, and closed her eyes as she saw again his expression as he said the words. There had been such strength and beauty reaching out to her just for an instant, almost as beautiful as love itself. And she knew then why she loved him.

CHAPTER ELEVEN

THE following morning Renata woke early. She washed, dressed in a comfortable cotton dress and sandals and made her way quietly down, and outside into the cool light of what promised to be a beautiful day. She had no regrets about her decision, but she wanted to have a little time completely alone to think about all the implications of what she was going to do.

She knew where she was going and walked steadily until she reached the stream, scrambling down the stony hillside to find a flat place to sit. There was such peace around her, and she absorbed it as she breathed in the fresh sweet air and planned how her life was going to be. She had intended to stay there for a year. She would be there for a year, perhaps, she hoped, more. But if that was all the time her future grandmother-in-law was going to have, then she would see that it was as rich and full and laughter-filled as possible. There were so many ways she could smooth the passing days for the old woman, and she fully intended to do so.

She was lost in this reverie when she heard, without surprise, Greg's voice, and turned to see him walking down the slope towards her.

'I came here to think,' she said. 'To plan all the things I'm going to do for your grandmother. I must see her doctor, of course, find out what she can and can't do—and we'll take it from there.'

He sat down beside her. 'No second thoughts?' he said.

'No.' She shook her head. 'If I thought I might, I wouldn't have answered you last night. Why? Have you?'

166

'No.' He picked a long blade of grass and chewed it.
'We'll tell her after lunch.'

'And then?'

'And then we'll make arrangements for the wedding. We
can be married here in the chapel.'

'I would prefer it in a register office as it's not——' She
hesitated.

'I know,' Greg said quietly. 'But—for her——'

'Yes, of course—it's best.' She looked up at a bird soar-
ing in the sky. 'She must think——' She stopped. An an-
nulment was not the same as a divorce. The deception was
for a very good reason. It had to be so. 'She must think it's
for real,' she finished softly. Then: 'Greg, one thing—my
father's debts. I have several thousand saved. I don't want
you to pay them off. It's something I have to do for myself.
Do you understand?'

'Yes, I understand.'

'So if I could still have my salary—do you see?' Good
grief, she thought, what's the matter with me? I'm stam-
mering like a nervous child!

'It will be arranged.'

'Thank you.'

'Any more questions?' he asked. 'About arrangements for
the wedding? Or will you leave it all to me?'

'I'll leave it to you.' Then she had a thought. 'The—
honeymoon—I mean——'

'Yes, I know. My grandmother and I share a small villa
near Cannes. We could go there, just for a few days, a token
gesture—the advantage being that it's quite private, and
there are several bedrooms. No one will be any the wiser
about our living arrangements.'

'And when we return?'

'There's a large suite of rooms upstairs—we'll move into
that. It has its own dressing room and bathroom. We'll
manage.'

'The staff will know,' she said.

'I'll show it to you later. When you've seen, you'll understand.'

'Will you take me there now?' she asked.

Greg stood up and gave her his hand to help her up. 'Of course.'

He led her up the back stairs, up again to a hallway she had never seen, and opened a door to reveal a large apartment nearly as big as some of the public rooms downstairs. There were armchairs and a settee covered in dust sheets, a table and dining chairs in rich mahogany, and the view from the windows was spectacular, framed in the deep red velvet curtains that were looped back with heavy gold cord. A door led off, Greg walked over to open it, and Renata followed. They were in a bedroom, sumptuously furnished with elegant cream furniture of antique design. Long blue velvet curtains swept the floor, matching the thick carpet beneath her feet. But it was the bed that she saw first, an enormous fourposter, at least eight feet wide, with white lace curtains drawn back on brass rails to reveal the richness of the cream tapestry bedspread.

'Good grief!' she exclaimed.

Greg went over to it. 'Now do you see?'

'It's huge, I see that, but what——' A glimmer of light dawned.

'It will be like being in two separate beds,' he said.

Renata stared at him. 'You're joking!' But she knew he wasn't. She shook her head. 'We sleep—together—in that?'

'Have you a better idea?' he asked dryly, and she was silent. She went over to the bed and sat down on it, looking across at the other side. It was truly vast, a Goliath of a bed—fit indeed for a giant.

She looked at him and he regarded her gravely, then lifted one eyebrow in a cynical invitation to speak. When she didn't, he spoke. 'A bolster down the middle? A sword —as in *Forest Lovers*?' he suggested.

She shrugged. 'Something like that.' She looked at her watch. 'It's time we went. I'm making an outfit for Christina later.'

'Of course.' He went to the door. There was something different about him today. Renata had thought so before, and now she knew she wasn't mistaken. It was as if, in a way, he were remote from her, aloof—untouchable, and she knew instinctively why. It was as if—she caught her breath—the 'marriage in name only' had already begun. She was safer from him—and from herself—than she had ever been before. And that, she knew, was how it was going to be.

She walked through the door that he held open, across the drawing room, and out into the hallway. 'Virginia?' she asked softly when he followed her out. 'How is she going to take it? Or is that none of my business?'

'It is now,' he answered. 'You heard her yesterday when——' he hesitated momentarily, and she knew why. Tension, of a different kind, filled them. A warmth, a realisation, a shared knowledge of what was past and gone, filled her very being, and she moved uneasily away, and he said: 'I told her we were finished, and we are. That's an end of it.'

'You're hard—hard,' she said.

'Yes. But what she did was unforgivable.'

'Did you love her?' she asked.

'No.'

'Did she love you?'

His mouth quirked, 'She loves Virginia. There's not much room for anyone else after that.' He looked down at her, not quite amused, not quite smiling. Of course he was ruthless, she already knew that, had known since she first met him. He would discard her just as easily when the time

came. The only difference being that Renata wouldn't
plead, or beg, or clutch at his arm, crying. She would walk
away with head held high, and not look back. That was the
difference.

'I see,' she nodded. 'Well, that's that, as they say. We'd
better go down to breakfast.' She gave him a cool smile to
let him know that nothing mattered to her either, and
walked on, down to breakfast.

The big moment had arrived. Lunch was over. It had been
a busy morning, Renata having spent it on her knees cut-
ting out material while Neil and Christina went out riding.
Mrs Masters had sat quietly doing her tapestry and watching Renata at work, and they had talked on various subjects, and the morning had passed pleasantly and quickly,
but now it was time.

Greg stood up from the dining table and gave Renata a
brief glance. 'Grandmother, I have an announcement to
make—shall we all adjourn to the lounge?'

She looked up at him, eyes bright with interest, then at
Renata, and Christina, and finally a puzzled Neil. 'Oh.
Well, that sounds interesting, my dear. Christina, pass me
my sticks, will you? Dear me, let's go.'

Greg helped his grandmother along the corridor, and
Neil, who was walking beside Renata, touched her arm and
mouthed the word: 'What?' but she smiled and shook her
head. He would know soon enough. What he would probably never know was that his visit had precipitated everything into happening.

Then they were all seated in the lounge, except for Greg,
who went over to the sideboard and fetched out five glasses
and a bottle of champagne. Renata, watching the old lady's
face, saw a dawning kind of realisation on it, and in her
eyes, and blinked back sudden treacherous tears.

Greg opened the champagne and filled the five glasses,

watched by an attentive audience. No one said a word. He would have made a good actor, thought Renata. His timing was perfect; the build-up was tuned to concert pitch, taut and fine, and he had the attention of everyone in the room—even Renata herself, and she knew what was coming.

He handed them all a glass, then turned to Renata and held out his hand, and she went over to his side, and he raised his glass and said:

'Grandmother, Christina, Neil, I want you to be the first to know that I've asked Renata to be my wife, and she's accepted.' He bent and kissed her cheek as an excited babble burst around them, and added: 'Please drink with us.'

Renata sipped, put her glass down, and went over to the old lady who sat laughing and crying all at the same time, the tears streaming down her face. Renata took her glass gently from her and knelt at her feet.

'I hope you're pleased,' she whispered. Her own eyes were blurred, and Mrs Masters leaned forward to kiss her cheek, and then took her hand.

'Pleased? Oh, my dear child, I'm so happy, so very happy!' She looked up. 'Greg, come over here.' He obeyed.

Clutching their hands, she gazed at them both. 'My darlings, I can't begin to tell you both——' she stopped, struggling for composure, and Greg bent to kiss her.

'I know,' he said. 'I know.'

Christina was dancing about, and when Renata stood up, hugged her. 'Oh, you'll be my aunty now! Do I have to call you Aunt?'

'No!' Renata laughed, saw Neil shaking Greg's hand, saw him turn to her, stunned disbelief on his face. Then he too hugged her.

'I can't believe it,' he said. 'My little sister!' He stood back and grinned at her. 'Let me look at you, Sis.'

'Christina, pass me my champagne, please,' Mrs Masters

begged. 'I must drink to you both, and your future together. This is the happiest day of my life.' She raised her glass. 'To Renata and Greg.'

They all drank. Time became blurred, the talk was nonstop, excited, full of laughter and tears, and through it all moved Greg, topping up glasses, smiling, the perfect host, the perfect husband-to-be. Mrs Masters decided that tonight there would be a special celebratory dinner, and she must have a word with Cook about it, and would Christina go and fetch her, and during a quiet lull, while Neil sat at Mrs Masters' feet and talked, expressing his own delighted surprise, Greg took Renata to one side by the window, away from them.

'All right?' he asked quietly.

'Yes. Greg, she's so pleased——'

'I know. Thank you for agreeing.'

'We won't let her down.'

'No,' he said, 'we won't. And tomorrow we'll buy the rings.'

'Of course.' She smiled. It was all going well. It was going to continue so. Then she remembered. 'But you're going to London with Neil.'

He looked round at him. 'Damn, I'd forgotten. Tuesday, then?'

'Yes.' She sipped her champagne. It was going to her head, unused as she was to drinking, and especially during the day.

'Tomorrow you can take Christina to York and choose clothes for the wedding and afterwards.'

'Yes, of course.' She was drunk, no mistake about it. It was the only excuse she had for the words that came out then, almost of their own volition. 'Nothing sexy, of course.'

Greg looked at her very levelly, voice and face cool. 'Of course not.'

She smiled. 'Of course not,' she mimicked. He turned

away and went over to speak to Neil, who upon the arrival
of the cook had drifted towards the other window and was
standing looking out. Renata stared into her glass. That had
been a stupid thing to say. She had seen the quick flash of
anger before Greg had turned away from her. No mistake
about that either.

She swallowed the last of her champagne. What the hell,
she thought. I don't care. But she did.

The next few days were a whirl of activity, of preparations,
of arrangements made, and planning ahead. Renata sailed
through them, her mind in top gear because this was what
she preferred, to be active, and not to have too much time
to think. She crawled into bed exhausted every night after
yet another day of feverish activity, and slept, invariably,
like a log.

Christina was wonderful. It was she who organised the
guest lists, who consulted her great-grandmother over
them, who worked alongside Greg and Renata as though
she were used to arranging weddings every day.

Both Renata and Greg, for their own reasons, wanted
the wedding to be a quiet affair, and the list had to be
pruned vigorously, but even then it had a final figure of
fifty guests, no less. The confession of Renata's true surname had, naturally, had to be made to Mrs Masters, who
accepted it as she was doing everything else, with a lovely
calm and certainty. Their greatest efforts were made in
sparing her from any work and excitement, and in this they
succeeded. She was an onlooker, on the sidelines, and perfectly happy to feel wanted and loved, but with no worries
about the complicated arrangements, and no part in the
frantic activity.

A week, two weeks passed, and the big day approached.
Because it would have seemed unnatural otherwise, Greg
and Renata spent several evenings alone, out in the car, go-

ing for meals to various restaurants and hotels where doubt-
less his grandmother thought they would be sitting gazing
into each other's eyes. They did nothing to disillusion her,
returning home sufficiently late for her to have gone to bed.

But they were like strangers, no more than that. Greg
had never even kissed her, or attempted to do so, after his
announcement of their wedding. It was as if an invisible
barrier had been erected between them. Anyone seeing
them out would have been forgiven for thinking they were
casual acquaintances, or business partners. That, in a way,
was what their relationship had become. He was courteous,
considerate and thoughtful on their evenings out, but he
could have been someone she scarcely knew. And of course
she didn't know him. She loved him, but she didn't know
him.

Two evenings before the wedding they went for a final
dinner at an old country pub which had a reputation for
the excellence of its cuisine, and they sat in a quiet corner
of the oak-panelled dining room, and Greg looked across at
her, and said: 'In two days we'll be flying to the South of
France for our honeymoon.'

'I hadn't forgotten.' She gave him a warm smile for the
benefit of a man who had not managed to take his eyes off
her since their arrival. He was sitting with two other men.
The diamond and sapphire engagement ring flashed on her
finger, and she wore a deep blue, low-necked evening dress
in swirly chiffon, and her mirror had told her that she
looked radiant. Only Greg seemed unaware of the fact. He
didn't even look at her as though she were a woman. Not
since that day. . . .

He was a cool controlled stranger, an escort, a partner for
an evening out. Renata knew why, but it didn't make it any
easier to bear when her heart ached for him, when her body
longed to be held tightly by him, when she wanted to hear
him say that he loved her. . . . But he never would, because

he didn't. He wasn't even human any more. Not with her, anyway.

'It'll be a rest anyway,' she said. 'And I can sunbathe all day.'

He raised an eyebrow. 'Not too much, I hope. We're not supposed to get brown on our honeymoon.'

'Aren't we? Let them think we made love in the sun,' she answered flippantly. She had already drunk two glasses of wine during the meal, and that had gone to her head because she had eaten little, only picked at her food. She saw his face tighten fractionally, and knew why. She had touched on the forbidden subject. She suddenly didn't care. 'You did say there was a secluded swimming pool, didn't you?'

'Yes.'

'Well then,' she laughed, and raised her glass, 'that's all right. *Everyone* will understand.' She finished the contents in one long swallow and put down the empty glass. 'I'll have another drop of that excellent wine, please.'

'Don't you think you've had enough?' he asked, very levelly—cool.

She pulled a face. 'Can't the blushing bride get a little tipsy before the wedding?' She picked up the bottle, but he took it from her and poured some wine—just a little—into her glass. 'After all, I won't be getting drunk afterwards, will I? Life will be very sober.'

'That's the arrangement.' They both knew they weren't talking about drink, or anything approaching it. They both knew, yet neither could speak of it. The gulf between them widened imperceptibly, and there was nothing anyone could do about it.

'Oh, how true,' she said, smiling sweetly, eyes cold. 'And I'll keep my part of it, never fear.'

'I know you will.'

They had that in common, at least. Their love for the

frail old lady whose life was now happier than it had been for years. And for Christina, who was blossoming into an attractive young woman. Renata stood up. 'I'm going to the ladies. Excuse me.' She picked up her bag and sailed out, followed by several pairs of male eyes. She smiled faintly at her middle-aged admirer. Damn Greg!

The ladies' room was down a narrow corridor, and she came out a few minutes later to see the man waiting for her. She attempted to pass him, but he blocked the way.

'Please——' he said. 'Please don't rush off.'

She stood there. She wasn't frightened, merely amused. 'My fiancé's waiting for me,' she said gently. 'Would you mind letting me pass?'

'The man you're with? He's your *fiancé*?'

'Yes. Now, if you don't mind——' She tried to ease herself past.

'I think you're the most ravishing woman I've ever seen,' he said huskily. 'I just had to tell you——'

'Thank you. Now——'

Greg was suddenly there, at the end of the corridor, his shape blocking the light from behind him, and the man turned, and Renata saw Greg's face, saw anger and violence there, and slipped past the man, walked up to Greg, and took his arm. 'It's all right,' she said. He took her arm from his.

'What was he doing?' he asked—and he wanted an answer.

'Nothing, honestly. He just wanted a word. Please, Greg——' She stood in front of him as the man came up to them.

'I meant no harm,' he said. 'I just wanted to tell your— fiancée that I think she's beautiful.' Renata took Greg's arm again. She could feel the tension of his muscles, sense the anger within him, and said:

'Yes, that was all. Please, Greg, take me back to our

table.' She pleaded with her eyes, and felt the relaxing of tension, and her heart hammered in relief.

'All right.' He turned and walked away and she followed. Seated again, she looked at him.

'Why did you follow me?' she asked.

'Because I saw him go out after you. He's been watching you ever since we came. Do you think I'm stupid?'

'No. But it didn't bother you, surely?' She spoke in calm tones, because one flash of anger now, or sarcasm, might trigger off the anger that was subsiding slowly. Greg looked at her.

'Did he touch you?'

'No. He merely spoke, said he wanted to tell me he admired me, that was all. He was quite respectful.'

'If he'd touched you, I would have half killed him.' He said the words in such level tones that the shock was far greater. Renata felt herself go white.

'Why?' It was all she could say.

'Because no man touches what's mine.'

'But I'm not yours. I never will be,' she answered softly. The words fell into the pool of silence around them, and Greg stood up and pushed his chair to the table.

'Get your stole. We're leaving. Go outside and wait by the car while I settle the bill.'

'But we've not finished——'

'We're leaving—now.'

Silently she stood, scooped up her white stole from the other chair, and walked out, and she didn't look at anyone.

Greg came out, unlocked the car door for her, and she slid in. The next minute he was driving down the road. He drove in silence, and she said not a word, because something had made him far more angry than she had ever known, and she didn't know what it was, and she didn't want to know. She had thought seriously about her decision since making it, and she had not regretted it, but she was suddenly seeing another aspect of the stranger by her side, one which made her uneasy and strangely vulnerable. Yet there was nothing she could do about it. She leaned back in her seat and tried to relax, but the tension sparked and crackled all around them, and she couldn't. She wanted to weep, but she wouldn't. There was an aching emptiness inside her, a sadness and a longing for she knew not what.

Greg stopped the car near the garages, and she said quietly: 'I'll go on up. Goodnight, Greg.'

'Goodnight.'

She flitted across the courtyard, a ghost in the darkness, and she was aware that he watched her go. Then she heard the car door slam, and his footsteps to the garage, but she didn't look back.

They were married. They slipped quietly away from the reception and few saw them go. Everyone was having a wonderful time; the champagne flowed freely, the guests had spilled out into the gardens and stood talking and laughing in small groups. There were several friends of Renata's there, including Diana, and her brother Neil—who were getting on famously, much to Renata's secret pleasure. James had taken the news in stoic fashion, had even sent a gift of onyx table lighter and ashtrays, but had, not unnaturally, declined an invitation.

Now it was all over. Renata had been moved, despite herself, during the ceremony when she and Greg had knelt at the altar—and when he had put the ring on her finger. She had caught a glimpse of Mrs Masters' face and the glow of pride and happiness that seemed to outshine all else had made it all worth it.

They drove away, to catch a plane from Manchester, and Renata looked back as the Towers receded, and thought, When I return, I'll be mistress of that. For a while at least, not for ever. She felt neither happy nor sad but curiously neutral, as if it were all happening to someone else, not to her. The feeling of unreality persisted throughout the journey; and the man at her side, who had arranged everything, and who was now her husband, was more of a stranger than ever.

A hired car was waiting for them at Nice, and they drove to the villa, in the hills beyond Cannes, up and up, along winding, twisting roads until they reached the open wrought iron gates. Greg drove through, then got out to close them, and she heard them clang together and felt, briefly, as though she were entering a prison.

The villa was simply beautiful, the sort she had only ever seen in glossy magazines or on television. Long and low, a sprawling building with red pantiled roof and cream-painted walls up which climbed wisteria and honeysuckle, and surrounded by flowering shrubs and tall cypress trees and a wild flamboyant garden that was scented and colourful and golden.

There were green shutters at the windows, and a long verandah with high curved archways beyond which were white iron chairs and a table. Renata breathed deeply of the scented evening air as she stepped out of the car. Soon it would be night. Soon darkness would fall and the sounds of the day would be stilled and they would be alone.

Greg took her inside. The floor in the hall was of cool mosaic tiling, the walls were white and covered with pictures. There was an air of uncluttered elegance about the whole place. Doors led off from the hall, and she could see parts of the various rooms. 'It's simply beautiful,' she said.

'Thank you. It's ours for the next four days. Make yourself at home, Renata. I'm going to fix us a drink and then I'll show you round. Come and see the kitchen.'

She followed him into a spacious kitchen that was lined with louvred cupboards in natural pine. There was a matching table and seats, and the floor was of red stone. Greg pulled down the flowered blinds at the windows after switching on the light and opened the refrigerator, which appeared to be crammed with food and drink of every description.

'The housekeeper stocked up for us,' he explained. 'We won't see her while we're here. The French have a very old-fashioned outlook on honeymooners—they'll leave us strictly alone.'

She sat down and watched him mix drinks. Ice in tall glasses, *crème de menthe* and lemonade, a twist of fresh lemon slice. The finished result looked deliciously cool, and she was dying of thirst. He handed her a glass. 'Cheers,' he said.

'Cheers.' She raised her glass and drank. It was delicious.

'And now food. Are you hungry?'

'Mmm, yes.' Greg bent and rummaged in the depths of the fridge.

'Ah, here we are. I telephoned and asked Madame Denis to prepare us a salad.' He produced a large wooden bowl covered in plastic film, inside which was a mouthwatering mixture of shredded lettuce, peppers, shiny black olives, prawns, egg, tomatoes and thin, thin slivers of garlic sausage. Renata's stomach protested at the thought of having to wait.

'Oh,' she said.

'Bread, bread—where the devil——' he looked around him, frowning. 'Ah, yes.' From a cupboard he brought out a cellophane-wrapped French stick and a bowl of butter, and put them on the table near the plates.

'I must admit I'm pretty hungry myself,' he said as he sat down.

They ate. The atmosphere was one of perfect normality. Both were hungry and tired after several hours' travel. They were appeasing their hunger now, and Greg had filled two more glasses with a dry white wine, and they drank as they ate. Soon they would go to bed and sleep off the stresses and strains of the last few traumatic days—separately. Renata was too tired to care anyway. She would have slept on a floor if necessary. It wasn't. After they had finished and cleared away, Greg showed her to her bedroom, a luxurious room with fur rugs on the stone floor and a large bed covered with a cotton lace spread in a delicate shade of lavender.

'This is the master bedroom,' he told her. 'Mine is next door. I'll bring your cases in in a minute. You have your own bathroom.' He indicated a white-painted louvred door in the far wall. 'I'll see you in the morning.'

When he returned with her luggage she was in the bathroom, washing away the travel dust, and he shouted goodnight through the door. She dried herself, found and unpacked her new nightie and lacy peignoir, and staggered, half asleep, into bed. She was asleep within moments.

CHAPTER TWELVE

RENATA woke the following morning to see the sunlight streaming in across the floor. She had forgotten to open a window, and the room was stiflingly warm. She had not slept well, which was unusual, and she felt still tired. After a cool shower she felt more wide awake, dressed, then went out to the kitchen to see Greg eating flaky croissants spread liberally with apricot jam.

'Good morning,' he said. 'I went down to the village for these.' He pushed the plate towards her. 'Sit down and eat. They were fresh out of the oven, and they're still warm.'

She took one. It smelt delicious. 'Thank you.'

'I've got the coffee on. Black or white?'

'White, please.'

It was all terribly civilised and polite. It was, of course, quite the best way to be. Since their wedding pact had been made, both had been drawing gradually further apart. Renata watched Greg as he went over to the stove, and thought about it. But then they had never been close—except on two nearly disastrous occasions—but she tried to put these out of her mind. Of course he was a stranger. He would always be. Their 'marriage' would be one of calm and mannered behaviour, for she had a job to do, one she would continue to do on her return to the Towers, and while to all outward appearances they would be man and wife, both of them—and only them—would know the truth. Greg might take her arm occasionally in public, or put on a pretence at fondness, and she would respond in kind, and no one would know that they were strangers.

She would sunbathe today, and perhaps swim in the

pool that she could see through the open French windows, and she would make Greg cool drinks, and see to lunch, and she would enjoy her holiday, for holiday it was, not honeymoon, and she would get home refreshed.

'Thanks.' She took the coffee from him. 'I'll sunbathe after, and perhaps have a swim. What are you doing today?'

'That sounds fair enough. Mind if I join you?'

She laughed. 'It's your place. Of course not.'

'Then I will.'

She remembered her remark, and his comment, about getting a tan, but she wasn't going to mention that again. All was going to remain calm. The memory of his overpowering anger was still within recall, and she had no intention of doing or saying anything that would cause it to flare. She had no intention, but she wasn't a mind-reader, nor could she see into the future, so she was unaware of what was to happen within hours. A seemingly trivial incident was to change her life — and nothing would ever be the same again.

Renata changed into her pale blue bikini after breakfast and went out to sit by the kidney-shaped pool. There were two lounging chairs at the side, and two lilo beds. She chose the lilo nearest the water, covered herself liberally with sun-tan oil, and lay on her back.

She heard Greg moving about the kitchen, and his footsteps coming out, but didn't open her eyes until he said: 'I've brought us a drink.'

'What? Oh, thanks.' Shading her eyes, she sat up. He leaned over her, wearing only tight black swimming briefs. She began to sip her drink, eyes averted, and it wasn't until he moved away that she allowed herself to think about his appearance. She was free to see him in her mind's eye, and she still trembled. Broad muscular shoulders, lean trunk and hips, long powerful legs. He was devastating. He lay on one of the loungers sipping his drink, a stack of papers by his side on the ground weighed down by a large stone.

'I hope you don't mind if I do some work while we sit out here?' he asked.

She could look round then. 'Mind? Not at all. Want any help?'

'No, thanks. I'm reading through some very boring statistics. If I do, I'll shout.'

'Fine.' She lay back again, eyes closed, half drowsing in the heat, hearing only the faint rustle of papers and picturing him in her mind's eye. A plane droned in the distance, and that was the only other sound. The air was heady with the mingled scents of flowers, lavender predominating. Renata turned over on to her stomach after a while and eased off her bikini top so as to avoid strap marks. Greg had closed his eyes and was apparently asleep with the papers fallen from his lap. She watched him for a few moments, drinking in the strong clean lines of his body, feeling a surge of helpless longing within her which she quickly suppressed. That would do her no good at all.

She put her head down, face to one side, arms and legs outstretched, and soaked up the sun. She was nearly dozing off herself when she heard a bell shrill in the distance, from the front of the villa. Puzzled, disorientated, she looked up, but Greg was dead to the world, fast asleep in the shade.

'Damn,' she muttered, stood up, and grabbed for the terry robe he had brought out, presumably to put on after swimming. It was too long and too loose and she had to pull it around her, but it saved her having to fumble with her top.

A telegram boy stood at the door, a grinning French youth of about twenty who eyed her appreciatively and murmured: 'Bonjour, madame, télégramme pour Monsieur Masters.'

'*Ah, merci. Un moment.*' She ran into her bedroom, snatched a few coins from her bag and went back. '*Merci encore.*'

'*Merci, madame, au revoir.*'

'*Au revoir.*' She closed the door and carried the flimsy envelope outside. It seemed a shame to wake Greg, but it might be important. She then made the movement that was to change her life—only of course she couldn't know it. She reached out and shook him gently by the shoulder. 'Greg, wake up! Telegram.' And she forgot that she was wearing only bikini pants with her robe, and the robe had fallen open. . . .

He sat up and took the telegram from her, still half asleep, opened and read it, and screwed it up. He muttered: 'Damn company can't run without me—I'll have to phone——' he stopped. He had looked up as he spoke, and she saw his eyes rest upon her and feeling suddenly self-conscious, pulled the robe round her. There was a moment's silence then: 'Did you go to the door like that?' he demanded, in a very strange voice.

'Yes. Why?' She felt herself go cold. His expression was suddenly like it had been that evening at the hotel when he had followed the man who had followed her——

'Naked?' There was no mistaking it now, the anger, the sudden blazing flare of sheer anger. She didn't like it—and her new-found serenity and acceptance shattered into fragments as her own temper rose to match his. Damn him! She had had enough of his male arrogance, being able to say what he wanted, while she swallowed her pride to keep the peace.

Her eyes flashed fire. 'Yes, as a matter of fact, this is exactly how I opened the door——' and she let the robe fall apart. 'Like it?' she taunted. 'So did he!' She twirled away and took a deep breath. The desire to hurt him filled her, making her almost dizzy with a heady excitement. She began to laugh, mocking, bitter, hating him for what he was—

then she saw him stand up, and stepped away, and threw the robe at him. It caught him round the shoulders and he tore it from him. 'And now I'm going for a swim,' she shouted. 'Topless—isn't that shocking? And you can go to hell!' After saying which she dived into the water, a shallow racing dive, and turned on to her back, her hair and face streaming with water, and feeling at last a strange release from the unbearable tension of his constant nearness. She reached the far end of the pool and stood up where it was shallow, barely to her waist. 'So what are you going to do about that?' she demanded.

Greg dived in. She waited until he was near her and swam away, swift and agile as a fish, and her own shocking anger was subsiding, for she had seen his face in that moment before he dived in, and it was like nothing she had ever seen before—and now she was frightened.

She was frightened and she wanted to get out of the pool and run into the house and hide, and she grasped the overhanging ledge and started to pull herself out, suddenly breathless—then his hands were upon her, pulling her back and into the water, and down, and she felt the violence of him, felt the strength of a man who had reached the end of his tether—who had reached the last vestiges of control and beyond.

She kicked out, lashed out at him as he held her, squirmed to be free, but movement was slower in water and he was far stronger than she, she knew that, finally, now, when it was too late. She could feel the unleashed power of his arms and body as he crushed her to him there at the side of the pool and kissed her with a savagery that left her mouth numb and bruised.

'No-o!' she gasped, but Greg had both her hands in one of his, and with the other, free hand he took hold of her hair and forced her head towards him as he punished her brutally, beyond all control. . . .

Then, subtly and imperceptibly, it became different. She was already trembling with fear, with the violence of his assault—only then, suddenly, so was he. She saw his eyes, she saw the pain and torment in them, and they darkened—then he released her hands, and he was shaking as though with a fever, and she was free to move if she wished, but she didn't, she stayed where she was, too weak to move, to fight any more. Greg closed his eyes as if in agony, then reached out to her, to touch her face, and whispered: 'Oh, God, Renata, forgive me—I want you so much——'

She put her hands up, so slowly, so carefully, to his face, and touched him. She was sobbing now, and all the anger had been washed away. He too moved, and held her and caressed her and buried his face against her neck and said huskily: 'Please don't be angry. I should never have said that—I——'

She held his head, cradled him against her, and the warmth and the desire for him filled her so that she could scarcely breathe. 'Oh, my darling,' she murmured, 'I want you too. Don't you know——'

Moving with great slowness, like a man in a dream, he pulled himself out of the pool, bent down to lift her out, held her, looked at her, touched her cheek, her neck, her breasts, as though he was seeing her for the first time, and was filled with wonder. His fingers were warmth and fire—then their eyes met, and they both knew what they had so carefully concealed, each from the other, for too long.

Greg picked her up and carried her inside the house. There was no haste, no urgency in his movements. They both knew that they had all the time in the world.

Later, much later, he spoke. Lying beside her in their bed, holding her within the strength and love of his arms, he said:

'These past few weeks were hell for me. Knowing how much I wanted you—knowing I was falling desperately in love with you, yet knowing what I'd promised——'

'You became like a stranger,' she murmured, smiling, her eyes upon him, feasting on his features and shining with love. 'Oh, Greg, now we know! I've loved you since— since the beginning, almost.'

He began to laugh, softly, joyously. 'Oh, my beautiful girl! You are, you know. You are a rare and special person—and I'm going to spend the rest of my life proving to you just how much I love you.'

He moved to kiss the tip of her nose, then whispered huskily: 'And I think I'll just begin again——' The rest of his words were lost. Lost for ever.

Harlequin understands...

the way you feel about love

Harlequin novels are stories of
people in love—people like you—
and all are beautiful romances,
set in exotic faraway places.

Harlequin Presents...

The books that let you escape into the wonderful world of romance! Trips to exotic places...interesting plots...meeting memorable people... the excitement of love....These are integral parts of Harlequin Presents— the heartwarming novels read by women everywhere.

Many early issues are now available. Choose from this great selection!